Snapshots in Prose

Snapshots in Prose

Richard Leonard

 iUniverse®

Snapshots in Prose

iUniverse books may be ordered through booksellers or by contacting:

iUniverse
1663 Liberty Drive
Bloomington, IN 47403
www.iuniverse.com
1-800-Authors (1-800-288-4677)

ISBN: 978-1-4759-3090-0 (sc)
ISBN: 978-1-4759-3091-7 (e)

Library of Congress Control Number: 2012910260

Printed in the United States of America

iUniverse rev. date: 11/03/2014

For
Geneviève Leonard
and
Jonathan Shubin

Dusk and dawn
photo-still
blue-gray time-
less foyers
for daydreams
holding us
in the breath-
less present
of silver
reverie.

Snapshots

Daydreamer 1

1945 3

Jamie Lachlan 9

The Great Escape of '51 15

Mother Superior 24

Home Sweet Home, 1955 35

Boys and Girls Together 50

The Summer of '59 60

Daniel Fitzpatrick 72

Brother and Miss Crabtree, 1959 85

Rosie and Diana 95

Garden of Eden, 1961 106

We'll Always Have Today, 1970 122

Daydreamer

When I peer back into my memory, I don't see a golden light. Not sepia, either. And there's no spotlight. I see shadows and shapes and maybe flashes of a face I never recognize. I direct the light, and it's always faint at first. I squint to shape the light, to focus. I am the lens. I see black-and-white grainy images. The past is the blue-gray of dusk and dawn. I never see much color in the beginning.

I'm recalling the images, and as usual, they're still. If they begin to move, I stop them. If I let them walk or run or turn, I'll never be able to focus their faces. And then I'll never see their expressions. If they're moving I see only blurs, figures in a mist. No, it's too soon for that. My mind's eye needs to see the faces first. I need them to be still. That's always the beginning. Again and again.

I refocus. Maddy is running in the surf, but I don't see her face. All I see is her moving shape, so I stop her. I hold her in place. I know who she is, because I decided to remember her. I looked for her. Sometimes she comes to me in a night dream—or when I see someone in the street who looks like her or walks like her. I enjoy that for a while, but this time I'm thinking of her. I want to see her. I have her framed photograph on my bookcase, but it's never so good as my memory.

But it is the beginning, and she's there. She's not clear yet. I stare and she is still. I see the outline of her face. Nothing else. Once again, she's posing for me. I'm the photographer. I recall the image and I'm developing it. I have called her many times before, and she has come. But I need to do this each time. She never remains focused. She always falls back into the shadows. My memory needs my light. But I have to think of her. Only her. If I want to see her again, I have to focus and wait.

Maddy's in front of me now. I can't tell if she's smiling or just staring back. But little by little, the lines become sharper, and I'm beginning to see her face and light eyes. She has short hair. I see no color. Not yet. Once she looks back at me, looks into my eyes, her face becomes more than the face in the framed picture on my bookshelf.

I want her to smile. I want her to be happy. And she is, because I will it. Before she became a memory, I made her sad. I don't want to remember that, so I choose not to. I also made her happy. I want to remember that, so she smiles. For me. She makes me happy. Always.

Now that I see her face, I let her move. We're playing on a beach. We're walking in the park after a snowfall. She's wearing her red beret and high boots. She's laughing. We're holding each other in a hallway. Hers always. I see the side of her face, and her eyes are closed. I don't see my face. I choose never to see it. Only feelings are important. It's the reason I choose to remember her. I want to remember my feelings.

Other times, I see images of loved ones and friends, and then all the others, lost to time and shadows, and I begin to see all their faces. Once I see everyone's face clearly, I'm able to copy my bright memory of them. I don't embellish them with too much color, because I want to be faithful to these snapshots from my past.

1945

At the end of World War II, my father found peace and beauty. He met my mother, and after six weeks, they married. The army sent my father home in 1945, and when I was two years old, my mother and I traveled on the Queen Mary to rejoin him in New York. My mother had no idea that an alcoholic was waiting for our ship to dock in December of 1947. Since my mother never spoke about her past, my father believed she didn't have one. She had a big surprise for him, as well.

His high school French was good for romantic dinners and long walks near the Seine. He didn't know that her father had died when she was ten, and that at twelve, she had taken care of her bedridden mother. To this day, she says very little about those four years. An orphan at sixteen, she moved to Paris to live with her older sister and her husband, who owned a small wine shop.

My father also didn't know that she had saved the lives of her brother-in-law and his underground compatriots in Nazi-occupied France. When six German soldiers came to the door of the shop to interrogate him, she slipped up the back stairs to the second floor, gathered incriminating papers from his desk drawer, and hid them between the newspaper strips hanging on a hook in the bathroom.

"Your *maman* saved our lives. She was very young but very brave. And very quick, thank God," my uncle told me many years later when I made my first trip back to France. My mother had never mentioned that story to me. My mother rarely spoke about the past.

No, when my parents fell in love, they didn't know each other. They were young and loved the mystery and intimacy of romance. The handsome American liberator with Paul Newman eyes met a war-thin Lana Turner in the wine shop. She was beautiful. The handsome captain returned to the shop several times before she agreed to meet him for *un*

3

apéritif at the brasserie across the street. My mother's sister and brother-in-law had convinced her to go.

That night, he enjoyed seeing the men look at her, and she admired his gentle manner and calm voice. She didn't speak English. He spoke French badly, but she found his American accent charming. She wore her mother's blue summer dress, and he told her she looked *très belle*. He also told her he was an actor and playwright before the war.

"Vous êtes un artiste?"

"Oui, je suis un artiste en Amérique."

He believed he would be one again back in New York. A colonel had promised him a job at NBC. My mother smiled, because she loved the arts. Before my grandmother was bedridden, she had painted pictures of roses on silk and played Chopin on the small white piano for my mother. She also taught my mother to paint and play the piano.

And Jeffrey and Renée married, because they loved all that was needed to know about each other.

Before the war, my father liked to say he was Brooklyn's Bogart, because he starred in *Guns and Nuns,* "a drama of vengeance and redemption, and the gangster whose high school sweetheart had become a nun." The play ran for two weekends in the Brooklyn church basement of Our Lady of Sorrows, where my father had been an elementary school student and devout altar boy.

On opening night, a local reporter showed up. He sat on one of the many empty folding chairs, scribbled in the dark for a few minutes, and knocked over two chairs as he left. He also had to cover a high school basketball home game that night. My Aunt Louise said the first line of the review in that "birdcage carpet of a paper" was the beginning of my father's "artistic drinking."

"Lachlan should forget about acting and playwriting, and get himself to a nunnery as soon as possible."

My father also wrote the play.

"Of course, like all young men with spirit and disappointments, he drank now and then, but that war introduced him to all that blood and French wine, don't you know," my grandmother always added. Gram believed that her son had discovered alcohol during the war.

When I asked my father about the war, he laughed and always had the same answer.

"Jimmy, if I heard gunfire up ahead, I'd jump into the closest jeep, yell, 'Get outta the way!' and drive in the opposite direction."

Then he would brag about spending his first year of the war in Iceland with the most beautiful women in the world.

"That was before I met your beautiful mother, of course, and Lana Turner has nothing on her." My mother has always denied the resemblance.

My father never saw combat, but he saw something that he had never expected to see—even during wartime. One night, in 1954 on New York's Long Island, where my grandmother lived, I saw it, too. During General Patton's Third Army liberation of the concentration camp at Buchenwald, my father and several other soldiers were assigned the duty of taking photographs of the rescued and the dead.

"We all stared, Jimmy. But we had to focus and refocus our cameras, and I couldn't stop shaking."

My father and I had been listening to a ballgame at Gram's house, and I'd been telling him about the German Luger Daniel's father brought back from Europe. After emptying his fourth can of beer, he slowly lowered the glass, took a long thoughtful drag, and ground his cigarette out in the full ashtray.

"Be a good soldier, Jimmy, and empty this for me. I've got something for you. I'll be right back."

He left the room and, a few minutes later, returned with a leather suitcase. He laid it on the coffee table, opened it, and took out a stack of 8 x 10 glossy photographs and handed it to me.

"You like war souvenirs, Jimmy? I'll show you a souvenir you'll never forget. Better than any German gun. Take a look, Private Lachlan."

At first, I saw mounds and hills. When I looked more closely, I saw bodies with crooked arms and legs. I pulled the photograph closer to my face. My father cleared his throat, and I looked at him. When I looked back at the photograph, I saw what I had not seen before. Naked bodies and skeletons with mouths open were lying one on top of the other. What was I looking at?

"Are these people, Dad?"

"Yes."

"Dead people? In piles? On top of each other?"

"Keeping looking, Jimmy. You like war souvenirs."

He took a long drink from his glass and wiped the foam off his top lip. He lit another cigarette and snapped his lighter shut.

I've always liked looking at photographs of people's faces in *Life* and *Look* magazines. And people doing things. General Eisenhower in a moving jeep and President Eisenhower throwing out the first pitch at a ball game. Jackie Robinson rounding 3rd base. Men in hats looking up at a foul ball at Ebbets Field. And why was Mickey Mantle smiling?

How was it possible that there were all these dead people in a photograph? I was nine years old and had never seen a picture of a dead person in any magazine or newspaper before. I had seen a dead girl, but I knew her. I went back to the funeral parlor to look at her. I wanted to understand. She was just a kid like me.

I'd seen her many times roller-skating in the street and playing in our schoolyard. Harriet Birch was in the second grade. Two below me. Her father owned the bakery with the round marble tables and small black-and-white floor tiles. Now Harriet was dead. Trying to understand that, I stared at her face, which didn't look dead. She was sleeping, but she would never open her eyes or skate again. That morning, Sister had said so.

"Eternal sleep. The blessed child is with God in paradise."

Every half hour during the school day, the nuns had taken one grade at a time to walk the three blocks to the funeral parlor on First Avenue to say Hail Marys and Our Fathers for Harriet. Since I knelt in the back behind other classmates, I saw only her profile.

After school, I quickly changed into my dungarees and sneakers, and returned to the funeral home. We were the only two people in the room. Surrounded by the heavy perfume of flowers, I knelt and watched Harriet sleep eternally. Whenever I pass a florist today, I remember her.

Here, in my gram's living room, I was sitting on a rug and looking at hundreds of people, and like Harriet, they were dead. All of them. But they didn't look as if they were sleeping. My eyes moved from one human face to another, to another, to another, and I couldn't stop moving my eyes, because there were too many faces.

"Who are these people, Dad? Why are they dead like this?"

"Most were Jews . . ."

My best friend was half Jewish, and Dottie, his mother, was all Jewish. What about Miss Bergson and some of my other neighbors? They were Jewish, too.

"What did they do?"

"They were born. Hitler was a maniac, a lunatic. He hated Jews, and he wanted to create a super race, a master race. The place was full of hate. When we got in there, the prisoners grabbed any German guard they could, and if we hadn't stopped them, they would've ripped them to pieces. You're looking at pictures, Jimmy. Imagine what those tortured people saw."

"Dad . . ."

"Get me another beer, Private."

I never saw my father drink French wine, but after the fifth can of beer, he did his Bogart impersonation.

"That son-of-a-bitch Hitler pulled the stage right out from under me."

Then he took a long drag on his cigarette, pushed the smoke through his lips, closed his eyes and—before the glass touched his lips—said in a low, hoarse voice,

"And he was a vicious son-of-a-bitch . . ."

After carefully placing the glass on a coaster, he slid a finger between his lips to dry them and took another drag.

". . . vicious son-of-a-bitch."

Jamie Lachlan

My father loved movies, and his favorite was *Casablanca.* When I was born after the war, he wanted to name me "Blaine" after Rick Blaine, the heavy-drinking, lovesick casino owner. Of course, my father's favorite line was, "Of all the gin joints in all the towns in all the world, she walks into mine." After he drank a few cans of foamy Schaefer, the beer of a "real Brooklyn Dodger fan," I knew it was coming.

"Of all the gin joints . . ."

When Nazi Major Strasser asks Rick what his nationality is, Rick answers, "I'm a drunkard."

I never heard my father do that line, which makes me laugh every time I see the movie. I admired Rick Blaine's honesty.

Of course, my favorite line was, "We'll always have Paris," because my mother was French, and I was born in France. But I was also very romantic, even as a kid, and I liked the movie's story of love lost, found, and lost again. Rick and Ilsa must part at the airport in the movie, so they'll always be perfect for each other. They'll always think of each other, they'll never change, and they'll always be lovers.

My mother said no to Blaine for my first name; therefore, my father settled for its being my middle name, which, of course, I never use. Not even the B. I'm surprised he never called me J.B. after J&B Scotch. After he drank all six cans of his beer, my father enjoyed a nightcap or two of J&B neat.

My mother liked the name "James," because her father's name was "Jacques," which means James in French. But she wanted me to have an American name. My father liked it, because Gram bragged that she had grown up with Jimmy Cagney on "our tough streets of the Upper East Side."

"Wasn't he a wonderful actor, that Jimmy Cagney? And he could outbox the meanest boy on the block, don't you know."

My name is James Lachlan . . . Jamie Lachlan. My father and Gram called me Jimmy, but my mother called me Jamie.

"J'aime le nom Jamie."

And that was that. I called myself Jamie, and so did everyone on the block and in grammar school. But not the teachers in high school. They rarely used first names.

"Lachlan, go to my office."

I'll get to Brother Shaye's being angry with me later. After my mother and best friend, Daniel, my principal was the most important person in my life. I didn't know that at the time, but I know it now. He gave me a chance, and I was grateful and became a good student. But I think you'll agree that I let him down.

In grammar school, I was a very poor student, because I had trouble listening to most people—even people I liked. I was able to limit my daydreaming when I became a teenager in high school; and several stories here are about high school and, more important, my relationship with Brother Shaye. For him, I learned to listen.

My thoughts began to wander a long time ago; it began even before I met the nuns in the first grade. I was very young when I began to dream during the day. Then it always worked in my favor, and it worked on its own at first. It protected me, because I became invisible. If I didn't hear my father, he didn't see me.

During my eight years of grammar school, I paid more attention to battles of war and cowboy shootouts. The bad guys always lost, and that made me happy. For Hopalong Cassidy, Roy Rogers, and the Lone Ranger, I'd stare at the screen and listen to every word. When they were about to draw their six-shooters, I slowly placed my hands over my hips where my pearl handled pistols were waiting for me.

"Slap leather or crawl, mister," I mouthed.

Hoppy was my favorite. He wore black and rode a white horse. He'd order milk or Sarsaparilla in a saloon and sometimes had to beat up a cowboy who had laughed at him for not drinking whiskey.

"What kind of man drinks milk, I'd like to know."

I waited for that line. When Hoppy knocked him out, he found out what kind of man. I wanted to drink milk, but it made me throw up. I was allergic.

Staring at a mean-looking bandit on a dusty street of a deserted town, I knew when to point my fingers, thumbs cocked, and fire at the screen. After Hoppy and I shot the gun out of his hand and wounded the other bandits on top of nearby roofs, I'd slowly move my hands back to my hips. We didn't kill them. We were sharpshooters.

"Winging desperados," I was also there in that saloon with Hoppy. Sometimes I'd forget that I wasn't. Sitting at my desk and pointing my fingers at the blackboard, I'd feel my ear being yanked around and around.

"Pay attention, Jamie Lachlan!"

"Yes, Sister." I quickly lowered my fingers.

"Are you sure about that this time?"

"Yes, Sister." No.

But usually in school, daydreams worked in my favor. When Sister encouraged us during Lent to get new suits and shoes to symbolize the resurrection of Jesus, I became invisible and thought about the peanut butter and jelly sandwiches we always had for lunch on Thursdays—or about my other favorite daydream.

War!

One Saturday morning at the RKO Movie Palace, my friends and I saw the Audie Murphy story *To Hell and Back* twice in a row. Back on the block, we got our authentic-looking guns, took our positions behind parked huge Chevys and Fords, and shot at one another until it was dark.

"You're dead!"

"You missed!"

"No way. I got you five times."

"They went over my head. I ducked."

We were bad shots and kept making shooting noises. Sometimes we got wounded and held our stomachs. Groaning, we kept firing, because the battle had to go on.

11

When it was getting dark, we made dying noises and went home.

"See ya tomorrow."

M1 carbines and Tommy guns. Tanks, flamethrowers, and explosions. Running and jumping into foxholes. Dodging bullets. Shooting Nazis. Hand-to-hand combat with bayonets. I could listen to myself think all day. I was more fun than Sister, and my grades proved it. I barely got through grammar school.

But not listening to Sister's pep talks about Easter suits didn't matter, because my mother couldn't afford to buy me one anyway. We lived in a small apartment, and my father never gave her alimony after "our divorce." He was supposed to send twenty dollars a week, and she never went back to court. My mother was very proud, so she didn't have money every spring for Jesus rising from the dead.

One year, I mentioned my needing a new suit and shoes for Easter Mass, and she said, "Wear your tuxedo."

"Tuxedo?"

"It's in the closet behind my wedding dress."

"You still have your wedding dress, Mom?"

"Never had one, Jamie. I guess you'll have to wear your Holy Communion suit."

"It's too small and turning yellow, Mom. Very funny."

"Jesus won't mind. He's got a good sense of humor." My mother had a good sense of humor, too.

Today, I still daydream, but I'm in control. Most of the time. I usually know when I'm doing it now. Thanks to my Aunt Louise. During one of our talks many years ago, she caught me.

"What did I say to you, Jamie? What did I say just a moment ago?"

I didn't know, and I had no idea that I had no idea. I didn't realize I was daydreaming, and I didn't know I wasn't listening to her. I was looking at her water-blue eyes. Her Paul Newman eyes. She had my father's eyes, but hers were never cold and never frightened me. I was thinking about that, I think. A lot goes on when I daydream.

I liked Aunt Louise, but she talked a lot when she drank. Even though she was never a mean drunk, I couldn't help myself. I drifted. When she caught me, she was nice about it. I think she understood the reason. She never took it personally, because she knew I was very fond of her.

"Where are you now, my favorite nephew? Come back, come back, wherever you are. You're gone again. Whoops, my glass is empty." My aunt also had a good sense of humor. I was her only nephew.

After that time with my aunt, I learned to fake it really well; and when I daydreamed in the upper grades of grammar school, I knew it and enjoyed getting away with it. I'd look right at Sister, slowly move my head up and down, and never heard a word. Thanks to my aunt, I was good.

In all fairness to the nuns, they probably weren't watching me as much as I was staring at them without listening. The classroom was jammed with fifty kids, and most of us shared a desk with another student. All the lower grades were big. When our fathers came back from the war, they made up for all those years jumping into foxholes, firing their weapons.

I did pay another price for being a war hero or a quick-draw cowboy during catechism, spelling, and arithmetic. I was a failing student, often promoted on trial. But that really wasn't bad for a boy, who was somewhere far away, saving the world with Audie Murphy and the United States Army. Somehow I was never left back. I don't think I learned much, but I knew how to study the night before a test.

I never did learn the alphabet, though. Our English alphabet. I know the letters. They were large and black, and right above the three blackboards around the room.

. . . L, M, N, P O, Q, U, R, X, W, V, Y, Z.

Knowing the order of the last letters was a problem for me, and for all those school years—with the exception of my using dictionaries and once taking a filing test for a college summer job—I got away with it. Maybe I just hated memorization, which got in the way of my thoughts.

Four times four
Shoot an outlaw.
A, B, C
Sniper in a tree.

The Great Escape of '51

Fluttering their eyelashes, bobbing their heads up and down, side to side, and undulating both arms on one side, then the other, the boys with the mean faces stood in front of me in the schoolyard near the church steps. When I tried to ignore them, their voices rose and they surrounded me.

"All the girls in France
Do the hula-hula dance."

Seeing their jerking hips "hula-hula" made it worse. Finally I pushed a boy, and two boys pushed me back, but Sister Theresa Thomas, my first grade teacher, separated us. She was very angry but never looked at me.

"Stop that singing immediately. That is very unkind. I don't want to hear that song again. Do you understand?"

"Yes, Sister."

"Yes, Sister."

"Come, Jamie. Let's go inside and paint." She took my hand and smiled at me. "You're a good painter, you know." I couldn't smile, even though I liked her very much.

When they sang during recess the next day, they surrounded me again.

"All the girls in France
Do the hula-hula dance."

They didn't hula-hula this time, but they hoarsely whispered the words over and over. I didn't understand them, but I knew my classmates hated me and wanted to hurt me. I hated them, too, and when I chased them, it felt good to see them run. Laughing, they ran to the other side of the schoolyard where the girls played. I stopped when I saw some of the girls laughing.

The next day, I didn't chase them, because they wanted me to. This time, I stared at the closest face, which was the biggest and ugliest, and tried to hit it. I missed, because I closed my eyes. I thought closing them tight would make me stronger, and the face I hated so much was still big and ugly in my mind. The laughter was worse than the singing, because I fell when the boy moved away.

There was only one thing to do. Stop speaking French and learn English as soon as possible. At home, I spoke English to my mother but insisted she speak only French to me.

"Français, Maman!"

English was the language of school and hula-hula, politics and survival. French was the warm language of my mother, of her affection and love for me. When she spoke English, I didn't like it.

After a while the singing stopped, because I made myself ignore them—and because Daniel Fitzpatrick became my friend. Everyone liked Daniel. And there were other boys who didn't sing, boys who became my friends for the next eight years of grammar school. But in 1951, Daniel became my best friend.

A month before meeting Daniel, I met Mario at a neighborhood daycare center around the block from my building. After school, my mother dropped me off there when she took an afternoon part-time job at the hospital. Mario was my first best friend. Together we could do anything, and we did.

Neither of us spoke much English, but we understood each other. We knew we were different, and so did all the other children, who never stopped speaking to one another. They didn't share and "play nice," and since our teacher didn't speak Italian or French—and spent most of her time with the other children, because there were so many of them—we saw her as one of them, but only bigger.

When my mother brought me into the large room filled with toys and small tables and chairs, I saw Mario and liked him right away. He was playing with toy soldiers, and he was sitting alone. When Mario saw my mother and me, he stood up; and with my hands in my pocket, I walked toward him. I stopped and he put his hands in his pockets. We were the same height, and had we the same hair color, we could've been twins.

From that day on, we never looked at the other children or the teacher. Mario and I were loyal to each other. We spoke with our hands and eyes, and agreed with nods and smiles, and we were happy.

When our mothers left for work each afternoon, we didn't cry. We let them kiss us and turned to each other. We had important things to do. We had serious games to play. We sat on the floor and prepared for battle. I sat behind my line of kneeling rubber soldiers. With his tongue sticking out the side of his mouth, Mario sat across from me behind his line of standing rubber soldiers. And the battle began.

We killed them with gunfire and explosions. Our snapping fingers sent the little green men with rifles tumbling across the floor, and they died with moans and shrieks. When we were louder than the children drawing at their tables, the teacher, who never smiled, stood over us and put a stiff finger to her stiff lips. Then she'd walk back to the other side of the room, which was the biggest room I had ever seen.

When all our rubber soldiers were dead, we took the silver metal knights on horses and those kneeling behind shields out of a box next to us; and making low crashing sounds and angry faces, we rode them off the table top. Even the ones kneeling behind shields rode off a table. This was better than playing war alone or reading the comic books my mother brought home. I didn't care anymore that my mother worked. I looked forward to seeing Mario.

One day, when the teacher was speaking to a crying girl sitting under a table, we played a new game. We put *our* stiff fingers to *our* stiff lips, tiptoed out of the room, and ran past the gymnasium, which was always empty, to the staircase at the end of the hall. The steps were high, and I could hear that Mario was breathing as hard as I was. We couldn't giggle anymore. On the top floor, we found another door and sat against it.

Once we caught our breath, we stood and opened the door and ran up the iron fire-escape stairwell. We were noisy, but we didn't care anymore. At the top of the steps and out of breath again, I used both hands to slide the huge bolt to the side, and together we pushed open the heavy metal door that led to a windy rooftop.

Under a cool autumn sky of sun and thick white clouds, we held hands and jumped up and down, and laughed. We had done it. She would never find us here. No one would ever find us. We made up this game by ourselves, and it was the best game anyone had ever played anywhere.

We ran to one low wall and looked down at the avenue. The cars and people were small and moved slowly. Even the bus looked small. I pointed to the red awning of the candy store, where my mother bought my comic books and marbles, and then to the bakery across the avenue. Mario pointed to two women hanging flapping clothes to dry on rooftops across the street.

We ran to the other wall and watched the lines of big girls and boys walk through the doors of the school on the corner. I saw our church spire up the street, but Mario shook his head no and pointed to a spire down the street. I turned and turned to find the park, but it wasn't there. I saw a water tower with rungs all the way to the top. Maybe I'd be able to see Central Park from there.

I ran to the tower and grabbed the rung above my head, placed my foot on the rung near my knee, and pulled myself up. Then I grabbed the next one and rested. This was harder than the monkey bars at the park, because these rungs were thick and rough. Breathing hard, I grabbed another and pulled myself up.

I stopped to rest and called to Mario. I looked over both shoulders but couldn't see him. I was afraid to turn completely around. I called his name again. I didn't hear him and didn't wait for an answer. I continued to pull myself up and stopped at every rung to rest. I was sorry I didn't have my winter gloves.

When I stopped to rest this time, I wrapped one arm around the rung and turned as much as I could on both sides. I still couldn't see the park. I could see more people hanging clothes on the roofs of other buildings farther away. This was the best game, and I had a best friend, and we had run away as far as we could without leaving the building.

I looked in another direction to see the East River between the tall buildings of the hospital. My mother worked there. I was here with Mario, because she was there. If I climbed higher, maybe I would see the big boats on the river. Looking at the hospital and the river, I reached for another rung, but none were left. I was at the top of the tower.

I wrapped my arm around the rung again and looked down for Mario. This time I found him. He was very small. He was looking up at me and waving.

"Mario, come up!"

Mario kept waving and calling my name.

"Jamie! Jamie!"

This was the happiest day of my life. When I looked up and turned my head, I saw the back of a building that looked like my home and thought of my father. He was probably not there yet, but I was happy to be far away. I didn't like him.

I was afraid of my father. I never knew when his voice would go low and heavy. But I knew it would. After a few cans of beer, it always did. He spoke French, but I never needed to hear the words. Through the cigarette smoke, the low husky voice and the crooked red lines around his pale blue eyes warned me. The change had come. I knew it would come, but it didn't matter. It always frightened me.

He would lift and tilt the glass to his mouth, but from above the foam, his eyes never moved from my face. I would become still. And quiet. He'd slowly lower the empty glass. Then he'd move his eyes to the glass, and we'd both watch him slowly place it on the coffee table, pick up the empty can, and tap the glass with it.

"You know what that means. Go get your old man a beer. Hop to it, Private. You don't want KP duty tonight."

I didn't know what KP duty was, but I stood, ran to the kitchen, and ran back with a cold can from the refrigerator.

When I handed it to him, he saluted, said, "Good man," and smiled. I saluted back.

His smile wasn't a real smile. It wasn't my mother's smile. It was a smile that made me look down. It laughed at me. As he slowly poured the foam into the glass, he blew cigarette smoke through his nose. Then he blinked his eyes and looked at me again. He always closed his eyes for a few moments before he said something. My smile wasn't real, either.

I looked down at my new comic book on the rug in front of me. Maybe he'd stop looking at me. Maybe he'd look at the radio and listen to someone ask, "Who knows what evil lurks in the hearts of men?"

But he wasn't interested in the Shadow or Jack Benny or any other radio voice. He was interested in me.

"Private, another can. Left . . . left . . . left . . . right . . . left. Double time, Private. You're on a mission."

My father's French wasn't my mother's French. It was mechanical with long pauses between each word.

"Look at me." I looked up.

Sometimes, between sentences, he'd put the cigarette in his mouth and blow rings up into the air. Smoke surrounded his head. He'd flutter and close his eyelids. Then he'd open them slowly. That meant he was going to say something very serious, very important. And each time, I'd wish that they wouldn't open, that he'd fallen asleep.

"Are you chewing gum? Are you? Throw it away."

I took it out of my mouth and held it in my fist.

"Why do you like comic books?"

I closed it and pushed it behind me.

"Big boys don't read comic books."

I didn't want to be a big boy. The following week, he would place all my comic books in a box, take me to the river, and throw the box into it. But my mother continued to buy me new ones.

"Get your old man another beer."

I ran to the kitchen and ran back.

"You're a Mama's boy, you know that?"

I thought of Superman on the cover of my new comic book.

"The army changes all that . . . Attention!"

This was another one of his games, and he thought I was playing, too. I stood and we saluted each other.

"Not bad for a Mama's boy. Say, 'Yes, sir.'"

"Yes, sir."

"At ease, soldier."

He had taught me to spread my legs and put my hands behind my back. If my mother wasn't home, he didn't stop. I was more important than his listening to the Dodger game. I was even more important than "Duke" and "Campy" and "Pee Wee," or the entire Dodger team.

My father talked and talked, and filled the living room with smoke and drank and made me listen. The eyes became redder and the smile colder. My father had very light blue eyes, and sometimes, I could barely see them inside the redness around them and through the smoke in front of his face. He didn't need to speak to scare me. His eyes scared me.

If my mother was home, she'd stop cooking or ironing, and call me. Then she'd take me to the bedroom and close the door. We'd sit on her bed and wait for him to leave the apartment or fall asleep. While we waited, we'd color between the lines, or she'd read my new comic book to me over and over. Superman was my favorite, and I knew my mother was not afraid of my father.

Now I was happy, because I was far away from him. I turned to look at the river when I heard my teacher.

"Jamie, come down immediately!"

I looked down. She was holding Mario's hand.

"Come down! Now!"

Mario was covering his face with the other hand, and his shoulders shook. I wasn't coming down. I didn't know what she was saying, but I knew I would be punished. I knew Mario was being punished. He was crying. I wasn't going to cry. I was never coming down.

I looked up and stared at the hospital for a long time. I'd come down when my mother came to pick me up. Maybe she'd come early today. Then I heard a man's deep voice, and I closed my eyes and hugged the ladder. No, I wasn't coming down. I wanted my mother. I wasn't coming down.

"Come on down, Jamie. You're not in trouble. You understand? No one's angry at you, son. You're missing a delicious peanut butter-jelly sandwich. My favorite, too, Jamie. Come on down or they'll be all gone."

He had a warm, loud voice, and I liked it.

I opened my eyes and looked down and saw two policemen. I looked at both, and the one on the left waved at me.

"Do you want me to come up to help you down, Jamie?" It was the warm, loud voice again.

Behind them stood the woman with the short gray hair I recognized from my first day at the center. She had interviewed my mother and me, and I liked her, because she said "bonjour" and "au revoir" to us. I looked for Mario and our teacher, but I couldn't see them.

"The nice policeman will come up to help you down, Jamie."

I shook my head no, and I heard a noise. I looked up to see a pigeon flapping his wings. From the top of the tower, he turned his head from side to side to look down at me. It made me feel good to see him.

"Jamie, we called your mother, but—*s'il te plaît*—come down before you hurt yourself. Mario is waiting for you, Jamie."

I looked at the hospital and the river, and then back at the pigeon above me, but he was gone. There was another pigeon flying behind a smaller pigeon over my head. I thought he could be my pigeon. The smaller one. They both flew to the other side of the roof, and they were walking in circles. My pigeon was trying to get away from the bigger one. Why didn't he just fly away?

I heard something and looked down at the policeman's smiling face coming quickly toward me. He was very close to me, and his face was red. I smelled my father's smoke, but when he spoke, I relaxed. It was the same voice as before, and

I wasn't afraid. Then he was behind me. With his arm around my waist, he turned me and placed me over his shoulder in one motion.

"You're okay," he said. "You're okay, son," and he carried me down the ladder and lowered me to the roof. He knelt in front of me and smiled.

"You're a great climber, Jamie, but please don't do that again. I'm not as good as you are." I smiled because he smiled. I liked him.

The woman with the short gray hair took my hand, but I wouldn't let go of the policeman's hand. She had to let go of my hand, so the policeman and I could walk together to the office.

The next day, they sent me to the psychiatric clinic in New York Hospital. After two days of observation and interviews, the doctor decided that I was an imaginative and sensitive child who had some anxiety issues. He had a beard and laughed often, but I didn't like him very much. Like my father, he closed his eyes before he spoke.

The psychiatrist also interviewed our family doctor, who was also a neighbor upstairs, and he confirmed the psychiatrist's diagnosis that I was a hyperactive boy with a strong imagination. My mother and Dr. Zeeman never told my father. I never went back to the nursery, and I never saw Mario again.

For many months after that thrilling day on the roof, I would look for my policeman. If I saw a blue uniform in the street, I'd stop in front of him and look up at his face. He would look down, smile, and say something, but he was never my policeman.

Mother Superior

One hot evening in 1953, when people slept on their chairs near windows or on fire escapes and spoke the entire night, my mother and I left my father asleep in his armchair by the window. After six cans of beer, he was always asleep by ten o'clock or earlier. My mother left a note under his glass.

"We are leaving."

We spent the night in a bad-smelling hotel across the street from the post office, two blocks from our apartment. The bed was half the size of the room, and the bed was small. There was a rusty sink in the corner, and there were roaches, crawling in and around it. The toilet was in the hall. The air was unusually hot and heavy for June, and the ceiling fan didn't work. I didn't care. My father didn't know where we were.

There was no smoke, no can tapping a glass, no red eyes. I wasn't a private here. I didn't have to stand at attention or at ease. There were no commands and no salutes and no missions to get a can of beer from the kitchen.

During the day, when my mother was at work, I didn't leave the room. My father would be looking for us. I had all my comic books and bubble gum, and I was very happy. After living there for a week, my mother came back from work with wonderful news. We were moving back to the building, and at the end of the month, we were moving to the second floor.

My father had moved out to live with his mother on Long Island, and we were trading apartments with a married couple and their baby. We moved to their large studio, which held no memories, and the other family was happy to have a one bedroom apartment. We had the better deal. My father had never lived there, so he could never come back.

As part of their legal separation agreement, my mother and father decided that I'd visit him two weeks every summer and every other Thanksgiving, Christmas, and Easter. There was more bad news. I had to spend the first two weeks of this August with him and my grandmother. On the last day of that visit—when I was packed to go home and excited to see my mother—my father refused to take me.

"Unpack, Jimmy."

"Why, Dad?"

"You live here now."

"No. I want to go home, Dad."

"This is your home now."

"No, I want my mother."

"She can take a train and visit. Tell me something, Jimmy. Will your mother let you have a dog?"

"I don't think so."

"No, she won't. You have Sugar here." She was Gram's dog.

"I don't care."

"You're going to be eight. Do you have a bike?"

"I'll get one."

"No, you won't. She won't let you. It's too dangerous in the city, and she's got a good point there. You'll have your own bike—and dog—here."

"I want to go home, Dad. I want my mother."

"I said she can visit."

"A boy needs his dad. And I can be like your mother," Gram said from the kitchen.

Gram was tall and slim, and was always cooking.

"No, you can't. I have a mother."

"Don't speak to Gram like that." I hated them.

I went back to my room and lay on the bed. I held the pillow up to my face, so he wouldn't hear me cry.

That night at dinner, my father asked me, "Can your mother cook like Gram? Taste those potatoes."

"You know, Jimmy. American food is the best thing for a growing boy," Gram added.

"We eat American food every day." Sometimes I hated her more than I hated him.

If it wasn't a dog or a bike, it was playing ball with uniforms in a Little League on a real diamond instead of choosing up a game in the park and using our shirts for bases. When I turned sixteen, I'd have my own car. Here in the country, I wouldn't have to wait for my eighteenth birthday to get a license.

"We'll build a hot rod, and I'll teach you how to drive now. Right here in the driveway. How about that, Jimmy?"

"Please, Dad."

"Soldiers don't whine, Jimmy."

I wasn't allowed to call my mother, and when she called, I'd hold the phone with both hands close to my face.

"Mom. I want to come home, Mom. Please, Mom."

"Put your father on, Jamie."

I handed him the phone and stood by his side. He turned, I turned. He walked a few feet away from me, and I followed.

"No, Jimmy's my son, too, and he's staying, and there's nothing you can do about it. Listen, you were the one who left. You took him away from me. Tell me something. How does it feel?"

I knew what he was going to do, and I reached for the phone, but he turned his back to me and hung up.

"Let's go watch dem bums."

He also had a television set, and my mother didn't. I didn't want his bicycle and his dog and his television. I wanted to go home. I went to my *own* bedroom, which I also didn't want, and closed the door. But I knew he'd call me.

"Hey, Jimmy, get out here. Jimmy! Private Lachlan! Now!" I wiped my eyes against the pillow and came out.

"Get me a beer, Priv . . . No, wait a minute . . . you're a private in New York City. You're Corporal Lachlan out here in this house."

"Attention!" Without thinking, I stood at attention, and he smiled. I sat on the chair.

"Who knows? Maybe we'll need a sergeant in this camp someday. Good idea? Would you like that?"

"I want my mother."

I was there a week beyond the two weeks, and there was a week left before Labor Day and the beginning of school. Gram was going to enroll me in St. Thomas of Hunting Place down the street from the house, but she needed my school and health records from St. Jude's.

"It's a much better school than St. Jude's, don't you know, Jimmy. It's Catholic, too, of course, but you'll get to wear a jacket with a patch near the pocket. You didn't wear a jacket at St. Jude's, did you, dear? Or have a patch? No, I'm sure you didn't. You'll make new friends. Nice country friends. Won't that be nice, dear?"

I didn't care much for my old school, but I had friends there and a best friend. I met Daniel in the first grade. He was never one of the ugly faces that sang the hula-hula song at me in the schoolyard.

"Will Daniel be there?"

"Who's Daniel?" She knew who Daniel was, and she knew what I was doing. She knew he was my best friend. "No, there won't be that Daniel there," she huffed, "but there will be nicer boys from good families at St. Thomas."

Daniel made friends with me in the first grade when no one else would, and when he did, the all-the-girls-in-France songs stopped. I was no longer the outsider, because everyone liked him. Gram wouldn't like his being half Jewish. She didn't even like my being half French. If she got to know Daniel, she would have liked him.

You had to like him. When he growled the lyrics to "Hound Dog" on the lunch line, even the nuns clapped. And Gram loved the nuns. I never understood why Daniel had picked me to be his best friend. We would go to different high schools, but Daniel and I were always together. When I let Brother Shaye down, he was there.

My only friend here at Gram's house was Sugar, Gram's black Lab. For hours, we played duck-behind-the-bed—which was a foxhole—jump on and over the bed, and attack the enemy.

"Sugar, keep your head down," I'd whisper and push it down.

I'd peek over the bed, and Sugar would raise her head.

"Charge!"

Then we do it again from the other side.

"Charge!"

"You're messing the bedspread for heaven's sake," Gram complained as she was smiling. "You two will be the death of me."

I tried not to think about my mother, because I'd often cry when I did. But when I needed to, I'd go to my room, lie on the bed, and face the wall. When I did that, Sugar would jump up on the bed, rest her heavy head on my ribs, and sigh. I knew she'd come and waited for her.

"Sugar."

One morning, Gram called Mother Superior, my principal at St. Jude's, and was very upset until lunchtime when my father came home from work.

"I have terrible news, dear. I called Jimmy's principal, and she said you and his mother must come in together to see her. Only then will she release the paperwork and his records. Those were her words, dear. 'Only then.' What are you going to do? She sounds very determined."

My father told her not to worry. He had made an appointment with the pastor of St. Jude's.

"That woman is not the boss at St. Jude's, Mother. Father Quinn's the pastor. The pastor is the boss. He'll give me Jimmy's file."

Gram nodded slightly, but her head stopped nodding when my father referred to Mother Superior as "that woman."

"*That woman?* Please be respectful, dear. She's a bride of Christ, don't you know."

I finally had some hope. Father Quinn was very good to my mother and me, but even if he was the boss, I couldn't see anyone telling Mother Superior what to do. My father had no idea. Mother and the other nuns were very hard on us, but they were also very protective.

If a man wandered into our schoolyard, a nun walked to him immediately. If he wasn't a father or a delivery man or a priest—if he didn't have a good reason to be there—the other nuns quickly surrounded him, and then all we saw were black habits around a head, moving toward the gate.

But Mother was the tallest and toughest of them all. She took care of the really bad students, those "possessed by the darkest evil," who were too much for "one of the good sisters here." When that happened, which was rare, he—and it was always a boy—was sent to her office at the end of the hall. We called it "Purgatory," because he didn't come out until he repented and his soul was cleansed.

Even though Mother didn't teach any of us, she knew us all by name, and there were many of us. Her different-colored eyes missed nothing.

"Joey, tuck your shirt in. In the back. More. That will do, Joey. You know perfectly well that God doesn't like sloppy boys, and He's always watching you." God also watched girls, but they were never sloppy.

"Yes, Mother."

"Jamie, come here. How's your mother?"

"Very good, Mother."

"Very *well*, Jamie."

There were stories of her torturing bad boys in "Purgatory," but I liked her. She was always kind to my mother, who spoke very little English at first. Mother spoke slowly and smiled during the entire interview in her office. We kids never saw Mother smile in the hall or schoolyard.

I told her about the lady in white who wouldn't take my lunch money at the cash register in the cafeteria.

"Never mind about that, Jamie. Tell your mother to keep her money, and you be good to her. You only get to have one mother. Remember, never go to bed a bad boy. If she should die during the night, you don't want to be remembering that, do you, Jamie?"

"No, Mother."

In bed with the lights out—if my mother hadn't forgiven me after my apology—I wore her down until she had.

"Goodnight, Mom. I'm sorry, Mom . . . Mom . . . Mom . . . Mom . . . Mom . . . Mom . . . Mom . . . I love you, Mom . . . Mom . . ."

"Okay, Jamie. I love you." She said it and meant it, and I fell asleep.

Of course, Mother Superior watched our grades.

"Study, Jamie. Your grades are not where they should be, and you don't want to worry your mother. She has enough on her mind."

She knew I wasn't a very good student, but she never held it against me.

"I will, Mother." I meant it, too.

"That's a good boy."

Since my father worked in a nearby lumberyard, he came home every day for lunch. My grandmother loved to cook, and after eating her meatloaf and mashed potatoes, or hot dogs with sauerkraut, he'd sit back, smile, and say, "You don't get food like this at home, do you, Jimmy?"

"Yes, I do."

I was angry and becoming braver—and my father never drank beer or Scotch during lunch.

"My mother's a good cook."

Gram and my father looked at each other and smiled. I gave the rest of my hot dog to Sugar, who always sat next to me.

My grandmother never liked my mother. My mother was Catholic, but she wasn't an American. And the French had "loose morals, don't you know."

My grabbing Gram's rear end while she was going up the stairs was proof of that. Sometimes, when my father followed my mother and me up the stairs, he'd growl and grab our rear ends, and we'd laugh and run up the stairs as fast as I could run. My father was always serious, so I liked his playing with me. My father rarely played games, and I thought Gram would like to play, too.

"Those people have loose morals, I say. Grabbing at me like that. What is she doing with that child?" My father never explained the game to her.

When it was time for my father to return to work, he'd ask me to walk him to the car. Today, as we were walking out the door, the phone rang.

"Probably my boss. Inventory time, Jimmy. He's got a drinking problem and worries too much."

He put his hand on my shoulder and winked at me. I wondered about all the cans of beer his boss had to drink to have a drinking problem.

"Mother, tell him I'm on my way back."

We walked down the hill to the car, and he said he'd be a little late tonight. Standing by the car, he kissed me. He was the only father I knew who kissed his son, and I didn't like it, especially when people were around. I didn't even like it when my mother did it in public, but it wasn't so bad.

As soon as he sat in the car, he jumped a little.

"Like the electric chair!"

For the past month, I heard that joke. That and the steering wheel was like a beautiful woman.

"Too hot to touch. Well, when you're older, you'll appreciate the joke, Jimmy."

I smiled to make him happy and wiped the sweat off my forehead. The day was hot for the beginning of September. He rolled down the window.

"Tuesday. Reserve meeting, Jimmy, but we won't miss Sergeant Bilko tonight."

He laughed and drove away. "The Phil Silvers Show: You'll Never Get Rich" was his favorite program. My father was a lieutenant colonel in the Army Reserves, and he loved anything to do with the army.

I turned and walked up the hill. The driveway tar was hot and soft, and the heat against my face and on my shoulders made me sad. Pretty soon I'd be going to a new school, and I thought of my mother's not making me do homework. I had just passed my aunt's house, when Pedro, one of her five cats, walked up to me. I sat on her patio and petted him until he saw a bird.

"He's a tiger through and through," Aunt Louise always said. To protect the other animals, she put bells on all her cats, but then they brought baby rabbits home as presents. Pedro was my second favorite cat, because he followed me.

My aunt frequently traveled to Mexico on business and loved the country. She gave all her cats Spanish names. Gram lived on the land behind my aunt's house, which was my favorite place when Aunt Louise was there.

I loved her, because she never said anything bad about my mother. I never had to worry about that. She drank but was never mean, and she could always make me laugh. Just her laughter made me smile, and she'd laugh even when she didn't say anything funny.

"Hey, Pedro, your mama's coming home in four hours." She called herself "Mama." There was no "Papa," because my aunt was divorced.

I'd wait for the sound of the five o'clock train whistle and run down the hill to her house, which was never locked. I'd wait for her in the TV room and watch something with Jose, Carlos, Juanita, Maria, and Pedro. "Cat Hotel" was one of our games. After a while, I had to open the door, because my eyes started to burn, and they'd all leave, except Carlos.

Carlos was a big black cat who got into fights at night. Bleeding and hungry, he'd come through the pet door in the back of the house. Aunt Louise would scold him and nurse him and hug him. Carlos was my favorite, too, because he'd follow me and even sit with me when I sat. I had Sugar up the hill and Carlos down here.

Today was my saddest day so far. This afternoon, Gram was taking me to the Buster Brown store in the village for new school shoes. I was really staying here. I gave Carlos a last scratch behind his ear and stood up.

"No fights today, Carlos. Be a good boy."

I was halfway up the hill when I heard something. I looked up at Gram's house. Then, I heard her. My chest tightened and I heard her again. I looked to my left down the hill, and there she was.

Standing on the other side of my aunt's house near the garage, she was waving at me and shouting.

"Jamie, viens! Viens vite!"

I ran down the hill and jumped over Juanita, who was lying in my aunt's flowers. Before I could hug my mother, she grabbed my wrist and swung me around, and we ran down the driveway to a car with its back door open and motor running.

My mother pushed me in, and because I didn't slide over fast enough, sat on me. Before I could move—and my mother could close the door—the driver looked at us and turned; and tires squealing, the car lurched from the curb and sped around the corner. The door banged shut, and we both fell over.

My mother pressed my head against her chest, and I hugged her. When I heard the laughter and shouts, I turned my head to look at the others in the car.

"We did it! We did it!"

They were laughing and clapping. I knew I was safe, but I couldn't stop shaking. My mother squeezed me. Then the car became very quiet. In the front seat was Ted, the husband of my mother's friend Leonie, who turned around and smiled at me.

"What's the matter, Jamie? You don't like being rescued? Smile."

"Abducted, Leonie. I'm pretty sure we're breaking the law. We're outlaws. But we're keeping him. Right, Jamie?" I always liked Ted.

"Smile, Jamie. You're going home," Leonie said.

"He can't smile, Leonie. This is Christmas morning and his birthday both on the same day. Right, Jamie?"

I held my mother's arm and listened to them. When my mother spoke, I watched her face.

"Thank you, Ted. And Leonie, thank you. Thank you, thank you, both. I'll never be able to thank you enough."

"Stop it, Renée. You'll do the same for me when I leave Ted." Ted threw his head back and laughed.

"No really, Leonie. Making believe you were a nun? I'd never have the nerve to do that."

"She's treacherous, Renée. I hope she does leave me." Ted laughed.

"From now on, Ted, call me Mother Superior. His grandmother showed me the respect I deserve." Everyone laughed, and I wanted to laugh but couldn't.

Pretending to be my principal at St. Jude's, Leonie had just called my grandmother to authorize the transfer of my school records. When she asked to speak with me, to wish me luck in my new school, Gram told her that I'd be right back from ". . . walking his dad to the car. Please hang on. Isn't this nice? He'd love to speak with you, Mother. Let me take a look. I'll be right back, Mother."

Walking up the hill, I saw Gram at the window.

"Oh, here he comes, Mother. Here he comes. It's so nice of you to call. Hello? Hello?"

Gram received no answer. From a corner phone booth, my mother, Leonie, and Ted were watching my father kiss me, get into his car, roll his window down, wave goodbye, and drive around the corner.

The rushing hot air from the open windows felt good. I hugged my mother's arm, closed my eyes, and listened to her beautiful voice.

Home Sweet Home, 1955

"How old is your sister?"

"Two." My father remarried and I had a stepsister.

"No, the older one."

"I don't have an older one." I knew who he meant.

"The one you live with."

"I live with my mother." I ran up the stairs. He knew where I was going. He followed me.

"Well, she could be your sister." He smiled. He thought he was being funny.

"Well, she's not." I hated that my mother was beautiful.

"Call me Jim. We're neighbors. We have the same name."

"No, we don't. My name's Jamie." His name was James Nolan.

He moved into Lia's apartment. He was a big man, and I didn't like him. I never knew if he was smiling or making a face at me. I opened my door and left him standing at Lia's door. His door now.

This was the first time I had to "defend" my mother in our building. The street was different. I saw men watching her, and I gave them dirty looks. I knew men looked at beautiful women. I was only twelve, but I looked at my dark-haired neighbor—when she wasn't looking, of course. I had a crush on Lia. But I never stared. I never asked her age. And when she asked me to wash her windows, I offered to do them for nothing. I'd do anything for her.

"I c-c-can do them quick," I bragged.

"If you slow down, Jamie, you won't stutter. Of course, I'm going to pay you, silly."

She gave me a quarter for each window—and she had five of them. She was the kindest, most generous woman in the world. Men in the street stared at her, too. She was even more beautiful than my mother.

When Lia married last month and moved out, James Nolan moved in. At the time, I overheard our neighbor down the hall tell my mother that he was a federal agent.

"The FBI has an office on Third Avenue," Mrs. Towers said. "We'll be the safest building on the street."

That was a strange thing to say. We were already a safe building. I never heard of anything bad happening to anyone. Once my father was gone for good, I looked forward to coming home. All the neighbors knew one another and said hello in the hallway, and they all knew my name.

"Be a good boy, Jamie, and help me with these groceries. My arms are about to fall off with these two bags."

The neighborhood was safe, too. Once in a while, one of the fathers got drunk and parked his car in the middle of Second Avenue, and we kids pushed it out of traffic. The car would be heavy, and it took six of us to move it, but we laughed all the way to the curb. In the morning, he'd deny being drunk.

"Nah, I ran out of gas."

Who needed the FBI? Who needed James Nolan? The neighborhood took care of its own problems.

My mother took care of our problems. At school, all the kids had fathers, and there were a few bad ones. Like my father, they drank. When the boys shook their hips and sang, "All the girls in France do the hula-hula dance," I became angry, because my mother was French, and we both spoke English with a French accent.

But their "where's-your-father?" jokes never bothered me much. I was happy not to have one. Unlike their mothers, my mother got rid of mine. They were stuck with their drunk fathers. And sometimes with drunk mothers, too.

Once my father moved far away to Gram's house on Long Island, our building was safe. He would no longer show up on Sunday afternoons with beer—or ring the bell in the middle of the night. One night, he stuck a pin in the bell, and it buzzed for an hour before my mother called the police. They couldn't arrest him, because we didn't have any proof he did it.

When we exchanged apartments in 1953 with another family, who wanted a larger apartment, I was able to forget the bad times there; now I was able to forget him most of the time. For months, when I came into the lobby, I'd look to the right at our old door. Then I'd turn left and run up the stairs to the second floor. But after a few weeks in our new apartment, I didn't look right, and I didn't run.

Our apartment was a very large room with a high ceiling, an eat-in kitchen, and a small dressing area outside the bathroom. I slept in the back corner behind one of the two dressers, which my mother used as room dividers. With a few round colorful pillows placed against the wall during the day, my mother's bed became our couch, the center of our living room.

I could read my comic books and chew bubble gum, because my father wasn't there to forbid me. If we wanted privacy, one of us sat in the kitchen and closed the door. I loved the hissing radiator and the smell of my mother's pancakes on cold Sunday mornings.

And I enjoyed the new view. Our old apartment faced a small courtyard in the rear of the building. Now, our windows faced the street, and I could hear and see my friends. I was very happy in our new home.

My mother gave me a key on a string, which she tied to the loop of my pants. I may have been one of the first "latchkey kids" in the city. Since she worked nearby at New York Hospital, she walked with me to school in the morning, and I walked the three blocks home alone after school, changed out of my blue corduroy pants and clip-on tie into my dungarees and sneakers, and met Daniel and the other boys near the corner by Charlie's house.

The street was alive with shouting girls hopscotching and jumping rope, and boys playing sewer-to-sewer baseball or touch football. When it started to get dark, I went upstairs to do homework and watch "The Adventures of Rin-Tin-Tin" and "The Howdy Doody Show" with Buffalo Bob on our new Motorola, our first television set. At six o'clock, I waited for the tapping of my mother's high heels in the hallway. When I heard her quick step, I watched the door.

Since my mother and I left the apartment at the same time in the morning, we followed my mother's rule of you-do-what-you-have-to-do *there*—and I'll-do-what-I-have-to-do *here*. But sometimes we found ourselves in the same place at the same time. That happened one frosty January morning. My mother broke the rule and came into the bathroom while I was in the shower.

"What are you doing, Mom?"

"I need something in the medicine cabinet."

"Hurry up or close the door. It's freezing."

"Just give me a second, Jamie."

"Mom!"

"Okay. Okay." She shut the door.

"Thank you."

I then heard my mother say a French word I didn't understand, so I knew she was cursing.

"What's the matter?"

"I can't open the door."

"What?"

"The door! The door's stuck. I can't open it. How are we going to get out?"

"I can wear your pants and climb out the window."

My mother's orange stretch pants were hanging on the shower rod near the wall. She made a face.

"They won't fit."

"We're about the same size, and they stretch, right?"

At the time, I was ten years old and small for my age. They were tight—and still damp—but I got them on. I opened the narrow bathroom window and felt the sharpness of the cold on my chest and face. Shirtless and shoeless, I slipped out sideways onto the cold fire escape and took as few steps as possible to reach the kitchen window, which was unlocked. I climbed easily through the larger window.

I ran to the bathroom, held the doorknob, and kicked the bottom of the door. When it was stuck, that was the only way to open it. The door couldn't be opened from the inside. In the morning rush, we had forgotten that.

My mother looked at me, laughed, and went to the kitchen to make her breakfast, and I peeled the cold pants off my legs. Shivering, I stood under the water and hugged myself for a few minutes to get warm. Now I had only ten minutes to dress and eat breakfast. When I walked into the kitchen, my mother was making her sandwich. She was smiling.

"That's very funny, Mom. My feet are still cold."

"Billy's mother just called."

"What did she want?"

"She said she just saw the sun rise in our kitchen window. Tonight, she'll have her camera ready for the moon."

Billy's mother lived across the street on the third floor. Sometimes she and my mother walked to work together. When my mother explained the entire joke to me, I was embarrassed.

"Come on, it's funny."

"Yeah? Next time, you'll be the sun, Mom."

Before my mother bought the television set, going to the movies was the adventure of the week. Every Saturday morning, I went to the neighborhood theater, where we kids sat in the front—without parents—and watched cartoons and movies. When the burgundy curtain rose, nothing existed around the screen. I saw the horror movie *Them* about giant ants in the sewers of New York City three times in a row.

But during the newsreel, or when the curtain slowly came down between the two features, we poked one another and wrestled on the thick carpet in the aisle. When the lights dimmed and the curtain rose for the feature—or the "flashlight lady" marched down the aisle—we scrambled back to our large seats and dug into our pockets for crushed boxes of Good & Plenty and Sno-Caps. Now, we were going to be cowboys for two hours.

39

Going to the movies *at night* with my mother was very special. I'd wear my good pants and shirt, and we'd pass the fancy Schrafft's restaurant on the corner to wait on line under the marquee. Once inside, we sat beneath a galaxy of twinkling stars in the ceiling, which my friends and I never noticed on Saturday mornings. I also hadn't noticed the oriental temple artwork, the gleaming chandelier, or the carpeted winding staircases on both sides of the lobby.

My mother and I never sat in the balcony where people blew clouds of smoke under the stars. We sat downstairs surrounded by hundreds of well-dressed older people. In those days, we didn't go to the movies; we went to "the show." Some people even called our theater a "palace."

One Friday night, about the time my mother and I moved upstairs to our new apartment, we saw Hitchcock's *Rear Window*. I thought it was the best movie I had ever seen, because I knew—inside all those windows on our street—there were families like mine and different from mine. I wasn't a Peeping Tom, but sometimes I'd look into a ground floor apartment if the Venetian blinds or shade was up. Seeing people sitting at a kitchen table—or seeing even their wallpaper—was interesting to me. I felt less alone.

In *Rear Window*, Jimmy Stewart watches his neighbors in a Manhattan courtyard, because he has a broken leg, and there's nothing else he can do. He's a freelance photographer, but he can't travel. He's grumpy with beautiful Grace Kelly, but she still loves him; and he solves a murder mystery, because she risks her life for his love.

To pass the time, he watches a dancer in her underwear practice her steps and a songwriter compose music. He watches "Miss Lonelyheart," a couple who sleeps on their fire escape because of the summer heat, and a sun-bathing sculptor. Like Jimmy Stewart, I found it all very interesting. Of course, the killer was the most interesting one to watch.

I wanted to be Jimmy Stewart. Even if all the neighbors didn't interact with one another, I thought they made their neighborhood interesting—and less lonely. They didn't know it, but they were all connected. Like frames in a comic book, their wide windows showed their stories, and I stared at the screen to know them. *Rear Window* was just as good as any cowboy or war movie.

As my mother and I walked home along the avenue that dark night, I looked up at the windows over the storefronts. I couldn't see into the apartments, but even the lights on the ceilings made the night less lonely and told me stories. If I were Jimmy Stewart, what would I see?

The old women and men who watched us play street games during the day were sitting around their radios or reading newspapers. Maybe they had a television set. Maybe the woman was writing a letter to her son in the army, and her husband was taking a bath in the kitchen bathtub or in a real bathroom. Maybe they were drinking soda or beer and playing cards. Maybe they were even thinking about seeing *Rear Window* tomorrow night. In those dark windows there, people were sleeping.

When we got home, I went to our large casement window to look at the apartments across the street. In some apartments, the lights were on, but they were too far away to see anything. Jimmy Stewart had binoculars, and he was bored. Living here, I was never bored. Sometimes I was lonely, but I was never alone.

I was surrounded by people who watched out for me. Two doctors, two nurses, a private school teacher, a lawyer, a movie critic, a private secretary, and an independent filmmaker were neighbors who took a special interest in my mother and me. They looked out for us, because they knew our story.

One very hot August day, my mother invited several friends over, and they had a beach party in our living room. They laid large towels on the rug and wore bathing suits. Since our windows faced only north, there wasn't much air. The small fan didn't help much, so my mother opened our door and the window directly opposite our apartment door in the hallway.

It wasn't a sea breeze, but the cross ventilation brought some air into the room, and her friends and she made the best of a heat wave without an air conditioner or an ocean. After ten minutes of jokes about sunburns, rolling over, sand in bathing suits, and beach umbrellas, our neighbor's head appeared in the doorway.

"Hello, hello, everyone!"

"Hello, Mrs. Zeeman! Everyone, this is Mrs. Zeeman."

"Hello! Hello!" Everyone waved.

"Trying to stay cool, are you?" Mrs. Zeeman asked.

"And getting a little tan. Get your bathing suit and suntan lotion, and join us," someone said.

"Oh, thank you, but no. I haven't worn one in years. But you young people have the right idea."

"Everyone, Mrs. Zeeman is my neighbor."

"Friend, dear. Don't forget good friend, dear. Well, have fun, children," she said and left.

An hour later, she returned with a pitcher of lemonade and a tin of German almond crescent cookies.

"Here's a picnic for you and watch the seagulls don't steal it." The entire building must have heard the laughter.

Her husband Doctor Zeeman was responsible for shaming my father when my mother and I fled to that hotel in the middle of the night. Embarrassed, my father left our apartment a few days after the doctor's visit, and we were able to return to our apartment downstairs.

When my mother and I moved upstairs, Mrs. Zeeman and he adopted us. They took us for long drives in the country for apple and blueberry picking. When I was sick with the measles and mumps, "Doctor" was my personal physician, and Mrs. Zeeman, a retired nurse, was my private nurse.

"Don't lock the door," she'd tell my mother. "I'll look in on him every hour. Go to work. Please don't worry, dear. I'm here."

Immediately after my mother left for work, she'd bring orange juice and a piece of cake on a tray.

"For the measles, you must drink plenty of fluids—and here's pound cake to soak it up with."

At noon, she brought her "special" Taylor ham sandwich with spicy mustard on white bread cut in quarters. Doctor and Mrs. Zeeman became my grandparents.

When my mother and I lived downstairs with my father, we met Doctor Harrison and Mrs. Harrison. They lived next door, and I knew immediately they were different from all the other neighbors. He called her "my Jane," and she called him "my Jim." Melissa was "our sweet cat." And I was "our big boy."

They were always speaking with each other. While she cooked their dinner, he asked about her day; and when he was doing a crossword puzzle, she'd lean on his shoulder to help. They even hugged and kissed in front of me. I liked sitting in the kitchen with them. They both had white hair and joked about their "artheritis," a patient's mispronunciation, which they found amusing. They were like characters in a love story.

If Doctor Harrison wasn't playing solitaire or doing puzzles under the orange kitchen wall lamp—or seeing patients in his apartment office—he'd read the newspaper by the sunny living room window. He had lost an eye in World War I.

"Let's put some light on the subject," he'd say and laugh.

Sometimes, sitting by the window, he'd watch us play ball; and if I met him in the hallway later that day, he'd congratulate me.

"That's what I call a home run, Jamie."

There'd always be arguments during the game. For a home run, the ball needed to go over the lamppost behind the second sewer cover.

"Listen, I got the best seat in the house, and that was way over the lamppost, Jamie. Since 1895, when I was born, I always had a good eye for baseball, and this one is it." He pointed to his good eye.

"I know a homer when I see one."

Doctor Harrison was my biggest fan. Like Doctor Zeeman, he had a broad warm smile; and like Doctor Zeeman, he liked my mother and was very kind to her.

"Never worry, Renée. He's a good boy, and I'm keeping an eye on him for you." Again, he'd point to the eye without the patch.

Mrs. Harrison was head nurse of surgery at New York Hospital down the street. Every day at the same time, I'd see her return from work in her white uniform and cap. She'd smile and wave, and tell me to watch out for the cars. I'd smile and wave back, because I was always happy to see her—and because I knew it had to be near five o'clock. My mother would be home in an hour.

Mrs. Harrison was Canadian and spoke with an accent. "Come to the 'hoose' for a glass of seltzer and cranberry juice, Jamie."

Sometimes we'd play hide-and-go-seek with Melissa and tap the wall, and I could hear Doctor Harrison laugh in the kitchen.

"What's that tapping, Melissa? Go on, baby girl. Go find them. Jane, tap a little harder. You're competing with a shadow on the refrigerator."

I loved being with Mrs. Harrison. She could be calm and serious one moment, and smile and joke with me the next. With her bright blue eyes, she'd listen to my stories and nod; and if I said something funny, she'd throw her white hair back and laugh. When she spoke to me, I knew she liked me. Her eyes never left my face.

When I think of her today, I remember the cold operating room where I lay waiting for the surgeon to remove my tonsils. I remember her bending over me and gently squeezing my shoulder, and I remember staring into her beautiful blue eyes above the white mask.

Summers on city streets were noisy, never lonely, and always safe. Playing tag, girls ran up and down the block. Across the street, the older boys played dodgeball with a newspaper wedge tied with string. When they accidentally hit a moving car, they ran away. Near the corner, we played off-the-point with a new "Spaldeen."

On Saturday afternoons, the older girls, preparing for date night or a parish dance, wore huge curlers under kerchiefs and carried grocery bags for their mothers. They ignored their brothers and the other boys who stopped playing their game to call out to them.

"I love your new hairstyle, Aggie."

"Meaning what, Freddie?"

"If you go to the movies, I hope the guy behind you is sitting on two phone books."

"You're such a jerk."

"Big date tonight? What time you taking your shower? I'll come up and cover your hair with a towel, so it doesn't get wet."

"In your dreams, Joey."

"Come on, you guys! Are we playing or what? Who's up?" That was Aggie's brother.

Every Sunday afternoon during the warm weather, the same two men in large rumpled suits walked up one side of the street and down the other. They stopped in front of each building to play their violins, and people clapped and threw coins from their windows. From our window in the courtyard, my mother couldn't reach them and gave me two dimes.

"Give one to each, Jamie."

I'd stand on the sidewalk and wait for them to stop playing.

There were three bars on our block. There was a drinking saloon near each corner; and the one in the middle was a family bar, where old men and women read their newspapers and books, and mothers held babies at the tables. On very hot days, the bartender gave sweaty kids cool glasses of water.

When the other men returned from crabbing at College Point, they'd boil them in the kitchen, and we'd sit on the bar's stoop and wait. Each of us always received a crab to crack against a step. Within minutes, there were broken pieces of shells on the sidewalk, and we had returned to our game. We always kept a close watch on their crabbing schedule.

After a long punchball game one hot August day, we were resting on the shady side of the street—when we heard the bell. But no one had money.

"How about a free cone, Mr. Good Humor man?"

He ignored us and pushed his cart around the corner. When we saw Tony the ice man's truck stop to make a delivery, we ran to the back of the truck for slivers to suck. He already had the block of ice on his shoulder and told us to wait. He'd shave some for us when he came back. But then we heard Al.

"Hey, get your water . . . melll! Get your water . . . melll! Hey, get your water . . . melll!"

Our favorite summer song made us run home to beg for money. My mother wasn't home, but I knew she kept her dimes for the basement washing machine in a vase on a bookshelf near the door. I'd scribble another IOU for that cool red slice.

I ran up the stairs to my door, yanked the string for my key, and shoved it into the lock. I pushed against the door and, hearing the sound of metal on metal, slammed into the door. I stepped back and saw the brass security chain we only used at night. Was I on the wrong floor? Did I run up to the third floor? Of course, not. I opened the door with *my* key. I tried to look in. Was my mother home from work? I was confused.

"Mom! Mom! Open the door! It's me, Mom!"

Suddenly the door slammed shut. I heard the chain rattle. The door opened and a short husky man in a suit and tie stood inside the apartment. He signaled with his fingers for me to come in.

"No, you come out." I stepped back.

"Please, come in." This time, he used his hand and arm. "Please, please, sonny."

"No, you come out."

He looked both ways in the hall and came toward me. Again I stepped back. He was holding a black attaché case. I moved away from him toward the staircase, and he pulled my door shut.

"Let's talk about this, son."

"Let's talk downstairs."

"Okay. Okay, let's go downstairs."

Looking back at him, I walked down the stairs ahead of him.
"Let's sit and I'll explain," he said.

He sat on the step, and I stood in front of him. He had a kind face, and I wasn't afraid of him, and that confused me even more.

"How did you get the key to my house?"

"I paid a guy ten bucks. I was supposed to meet a woman in there. You know."

"What woman?"

I thought of my mother. Was someone playing a trick on her? Not even my father. He wouldn't do that.

"You know . . . sex."

"What? My mother? Who gave you the key?"

"No, no. Not your mother. Some young girl. A teenage girl, you know. I was supposed to meet some young girl . . . and give these presents I brought." He looked at the attaché case on the step next to him.

"You know, girl things. You know. For a young gir . . ."

We both heard the key turn a lock and looked toward the building's hallway door. It was near noon, and James Dolan was coming home for lunch, something he did often, since the FBI building was only three blocks away.

"James?" I had never used his name, so he looked surprised.

"This man was in my apartment."

Then James didn't look surprised. He looked hard and cold. He walked to us and stood over the man. The man looked up at him, and James took out his wallet and showed him something.

"Open that. Now."

"Why? There's nothing . . ."

"Open it." The man opened it, and we all looked down.

"That's my Brownie camera, and that's my mother's bracelet, and that's . . ."

Suddenly the man stood and pushed past James, but James grabbed the back of his jacket collar, and I grabbed the man's arm. He fell to his knee, and James swung his fist down and punched him in the side of his face. I stepped back.

But the man quickly stood up, and James, who was much taller, swung down again and punched the other side of his face. Again and again, he punched the man's face and back, but the man continued to stand. I was beginning to feel sorry for him.

"Stay down. Please," I said. James said nothing.

The man was down on one knee and looked at me for a moment. Then, with his head down like a football player, he ran between James and me to the staircase, which surprised me. Where was he going? James grabbed his arm and punched him twice in the back, and I heard the man grunt. But he continued to run up the stairs.

There were drops of blood splattered on the stairs and wall. James slipped on a first step. I heard him curse, but he was fast and caught the man on the landing between my floor and the third floor.

James shoved the man down into a corner. He raised his fist above the man. The man's face was red and bloody, and his tie was over his shoulder. We were all breathing hard.

Then this man, who was soft spoken in the lobby, growled, "Go ahead, big shot. Hit me again."

James pulled his coat back for the man to see a gun on his hip.

"You move and you're dead."

Neither man said another word, and I hoped he wouldn't move. This was not the movies, and I was shaking.

"Call the police."

I didn't realize James was speaking to me.

"Now. Call the police."

When the police arrived, they questioned James and me, and I told them that the burglar had never hurt me. He could have pulled me into the apartment. He could have punched me in the hall. He was a strong man. I knew that now. And he was much bigger than I was. Had he hit me and knocked me down, he'd be free. No, even when James was beating him, he never tried to hit us back.

I asked the police for the key he had used. They smiled and showed me the burglary tools. They told me he was a professional, who broke into apartments only during the day to "avoid violent situations like this one." Knowing the laws he was breaking, he chose to break the less serious ones.

To the police officer—in front of the man—I said, "He never hurt me. He could have." I wanted the burglar to know that I was grateful.

I never found out what had happened to him. There was never a trial. The district attorney asked my mother if she wanted to press additional charges, and my mother answered, "No. He never hurt my son."

A year later, I saw the burglar on a Third Avenue bus. When he saw me, he immediately pulled the bell rope and got off at the next stop. I looked out the window and saw him on the sidewalk. Looking away from my bus, he was waiting for another one.

In 1961, they demolished the RKO movie theater, our palace, and built a huge white apartment building, and I was now in high school. The year before, James was transferred to Dallas where he became the new bureau chief. At the time, Mrs. Towers told my mother that all the neighbors would miss him.

"He's a hero, isn't he?"

And the burglar. He was nothing like the killer in *Rear Window*, but he changed my building forever.

Boys and Girls Together

Although Mother Superior and all the other sisters were very kind to my mother and me when we had that abduction problem with my father, some of them found fifty kids in one classroom twenty too many; and they let us boys know it. They were never angry with the girls. I understood. I knew girls were better students. But I also believed ten-year-old boys were more fun. You would never see a girl play tug-of-war with a nun in grammar school.

"No." The pointer and Sister's arm moved up and down, side to side.

"Let go, Andy."

"No."

"Andy! I said let go!"

Sister was tugging and shaking the pointer back and forth, up and down, but Andy never moved. From my seat in the back, it looked as if he were jerking Sister around the front of the room with the flick of his wrist. Up and down, back and forth, this way and that way.

"Andy, let go immediately!"

"That hurt, Sister."

His voice was low. Too low for a big kid. I never heard Andy raise his voice, but I wondered if he was going to cry. Andy never cried.

"Andy!"

"No, you're going to hit me again."

"I won't, Andy. Let go. Now!"

Her voice was very loud for a small nun. Andy was three heads taller than Lampshade. We called Sister, "Lampshade," because she was short and wide—and her habit, covering her feet, looked like a black-and-white lampshade.

Andy was the biggest kid in class, because he was left back once or twice. Andy was also the nicest kid in class. He never "ranked" on parents, something we always did to one another.

"What happened to your mama's teeth? She lose them in an apple or what?"

"You gonna be a *druuunk* like your father?"

"Mama, where's Papa?"

That last one was about me. I was the only one in class with divorced parents.

"You won't hit me again, Sister?"

"Andy!"

"Promise?"

"Yes, yes."

Andy let go of the pointer, and when he turned to walk back to his desk, we heard it.

Whack!

Andy should have made her swear on a Bible. She hit him on the head. Once we realized what had happened, we slapped our desks and laughed. We liked Andy, but that was funny. He looked so surprised. And it even made a funny sound. A hollow sound.

Whack!

Sister snapped the pointer up, but Andy ran out of the room. He was also the fastest kid in the class, and holding his head with two hands didn't slow him down. He was so fast that Sister swung again, this time hitting the bottom of her habit and the floor. Looking at the empty doorway, we laughed again.

We listened to Andy run down the usually quiet hall, and then we heard the heavy wooden doors to the street slam open against the wall and slam shut. Even some of the girls laughed. When we looked at Sister, we all stopped laughing. Lampshade was looking at us. She didn't punish us, I guess, because the girls had been laughing, too.

Watching ourselves "get the pointer" was funny, because every day we boys got hit; and our making faces and jumping up and down made us look like Tom and Jerry cartoons—or

Jerry Lewis, whose movies always made me laugh. And watching certain friends get hit was always better than reciting catechism and doing arithmetic.

If we were called up to be hit, we'd hurry to be first in line, then hurry back to our desks, blow into hot-stinging red hands, and laugh at our friends who made the best faces. If the line was long, we had favorites.

Timmy was the funniest, because he'd scream just before the pointer hit his hand. The first time he did it, he surprised Sister, and I think she smiled a little. She didn't hit him that time, but she never smiled again.

With our elbows on the desks, we'd lean forward in our seats and wait for Timmy to stick out his hand—and he was on line almost every day. He was always in trouble. Timmy had a death wish, but he made school fun. He could have been on Sid Caesar's "Your Show of Shows" or "I Love Lucy."

On the first day of 5th grade, he hid in the coat closet before Sister began taking attendance.

"Timmy?"

"Here, Sister!" She looked at his empty seat.

"Timmy? Where are you, Timmy?" She knew about Timmy, because everyone at school knew about him.

"Right in front of you, Sister."

She walked to his desk, which was next to the closet. Timmy would do this to Sister Margaret Anthony last year, and she'd laugh. She never hit anyone, even when we deserved it. I liked her very much, but she was too nice, and we took advantage of that. Sister Margaret Anthony couldn't handle the boys. There were too many of us, and we were bad.

This year, we had Sister Mary John. We called her "Hatchet Face," because she chopped at our hands with the pointer. I never thought her face looked like a hatchet, but that's what the older kids called her. Timmy really wanted a *painful* death.

"Where are you, Timmy?" He didn't yell this time.

"Here," he said in a church voice.

He knew she was near. When she kicked the door, it slid open; and sitting on the floor, Timmy waved his hand in front of his face.

"Here."

Timmy must have had cat lives. Nothing happened. That time.

When he was caught imitating Elvis and shaking his hips on line for weekly confession, he didn't get away with it. That must have been a sin, because Sister dragged him out of church by his hair. I laughed so hard I forgot most of my weekly sins: lied to my mother, cursed ten times, stole a dime from the laundry money for watermelon, looked at a dirty picture in the Public Library . . .

Another time, he pulled his hand away just as Sister came down with the pointer, and she put one hand on her hip and tapped Timmy's head with the pointer.

"You're making it harder on yourself, Timmy. Don't pull your hand away, or you'll get two."

"I didn't do it, Sister."

"Who did? The Holy Ghost?"

"I don't know, Sister. My eyes were closed." We always waited for Timmy.

The year Sister Mary Thomas hit Helen Reilly, we didn't laugh. We'd never seen a girl get hit; and during my eight years at St. Jude's, Helen was the only girl I ever saw get hit. There were two things that separated us from them. Most girls were smarter than most of us; a girl usually won the spelling bee and the current event challenge on Thursdays and Fridays. I never got past the second round.

"No. Sit down, Jamie." I never cared.

And girls were never punished. Except Helen. Sister smacked her face so hard, her legs folded and she fell against the blackboard. When she ran back to her seat with her hands holding her face—and then sat at her desk crying into her folded arms—we didn't laugh. We couldn't believe Sister had hit a girl. The room was so quiet, we could hear Sister's rosary beads clinking and Helen's trying to catch her breath.

We never found out what Helen had done in the sixth grade that was so awful. Girls never punched girls next to them, or took God's name in vain, or cheated on tests. Girls always raised their hands, and I never saw them copy their friends' homework in the schoolyard. Girls didn't throw paper airplanes. I never even saw a girl being scolded.

"Something in the hand means nothing in the brain." Sister was talking to one of us.

Girls did pass notes but never got caught. And like the sisters, girls had good penmanship.

I don't think the girls even knew what Helen had done. Like us, they looked surprised. I never saw a girl get into trouble, but some of them enjoyed it when we had. Going back to my seat after getting my knuckles rapped or my ears clapped, I'd see a smile here and there.

When Helen ran back to her seat, no one laughed. I looked around the room, and I don't think any girl even smiled. Quietly we just listened to Helen and watched Sister, who was looking at Helen. I thought I'd be happy to see a girl get hit for once, but I wasn't. I felt sorry for her.

Maybe the girls found out later, but I didn't speak with many of them. We never bothered with one another during recess, and none of them lived on my block. I had only one friend who was a girl, and she didn't go to St. Jude's. Donna lived on the block, and we met when we were ten. She taught me how to ride a two-wheeler. She was the only kid on the street with a bike, which she shared with her kid brother, Eddie.

With her blonde ponytail flapping behind her, she could outskate all of us. She could even roller skate on the avenue's cobblestones. Her mother owned "Mary's," the small grocery store on the street, and gave all the kids credit up to a dollar. In the winter, she let us put our wet gloves on the wooden board above the radiator after a snowball war, and the store smelled like wool.

Donna and I were good friends. I think she may have had a crush on me. She'd call up to my window for me to "come down and play," and she always sat next to me on her fire escape or stoop, and gave me slugs of her Mission Grape soda; she gave only sips to the other kids. After I gave her the bottle back, she never wiped it clean with her hand or shirt. She drank from it right away. She wanted me to see that.

Years later, she was my high school prom date. I didn't have a girlfriend. She offered to pay for herself, but I said no. She was my date. I don't think her steady boyfriend was happy about it, but she didn't care. She told him that we grew up together. She probably didn't mention her calling up to my window Saturday mornings and the slugs of soda on her fire escape.

Growing up on the block, Donna was my only good "girl friend." She was never a girlfriend. In school, I had no good girl friend, but I did feel something different around one girl, and I hardly knew her. I knew that butterfly feeling well, because I had it when my next door neighbor Lia spoke to me.

Lia was a runway model. She was tall and thin, and had dark skin and light green eyes; and whenever she saw me and smiled, her eyes sparkled. If I was standing across the street on the corner with my friends, she'd smile and wave. Of course, that made me a big shot, because everyone watched Lia walk up and down the street. I think the girls watched her more than we did.

"Look at that walk. She thinks who she is."

When Lia and I met in the hallway, I'd stutter, because I was a stutterer when I was nervous—and I really didn't want to stutter then, which made it even worse. She'd put her hand on my shoulder and smile.

"You're speaking too quickly, Jamie. Please slow down, honey." I'd speak slowly and stop stuttering.

Then she'd smile and say, "See?"

But I'd stutter again the next time we met in the hallway, and she'd be sweet again. I knew she was too old and just being nice, but it was exciting being near Lia. She always gave me butterflies.

One day in the school lunchroom, Bonnie, who didn't look anything like Lia, because she was short and pencil skinny, covered my eyes with her hands and ran back to her table of giggling girlfriends staring at me. No girl had ever touched my face like that before, and I couldn't stop thinking about that and the way she had said,

"Guess who, Jamie Lachlan."

When she covered my eyes, I was about to take a bite of my sandwich. Daniel and my other friends laughed, and I put it down, turned, and looked for her table. She and her friends were sitting near the bathrooms. Her friends knew she was going to do it. When she ran back to them, they all reached across the table and held her hand. Daniel told me so. Maybe it was just a dare. But why had she picked me? I couldn't finish my sandwich, which was the Tuesday special, and I liked baloney.

From that day on, Bonnie was beautiful and her voice was different, sweet and clear, and I listened to her answers in class. I never enjoyed catechism so much. She sat near the side blackboard in front of me, so I could watch her, but she would need to turn in her seat to catch me. Sometimes she did and smiled, but I'd quickly shift my eyes to an alphabet letter above the blackboard behind her. When it was safe, I'd look at her again.

Listening to her voice or watching her take notes from the blackboard and write in her notebook was better than watching dust float in afternoon sun bars—or playing "war," jabbing small drawings of German airplanes over an empty inkwell hole with a sharp pencil. Lying in bed at night, I thought about Bonnie touching my face, so I would dream about her when I fell asleep, and sometimes it worked.

They were always the same two dreams. Playing roller hockey in the park near school, I scored a goal. Or I'd hit a home run, winning the Yorkville Softball Tournament. Bonnie was always there, standing behind the chain link fence, watching me, smiling for me while I skated around the net or crossed home plate. I'd look at her but never smile back, because heroes are always humble.

After dinner I'd lie on my bed and wait for songs like "Earth Angel" and "Goodnight Sweetheart" on WINS radio, so I could see those scenes over and over. I wanted to see her face through the fence. I wanted to see her covering my eyes or turning to look at me in class. When my mother finished the dishes, I'd turn the light on and the radio off.

Maybe it was just a dare, but I enjoyed going to school and listening in class for a while. Maybe it wasn't a dare. She never covered another boy's eyes in the cafeteria. I know. I changed my seat and watched. But I was shy and never spoke to Bonnie in the schoolyard; and when her parents moved downtown at the end of the year, she went to another school. Bonnie was gone for good, and I stopped lying on my bed after dinner.

Flying outside the classroom windows, a Messerschmitt was attacking the school again, and I sharpened my pencil.

When we were older kids, the sisters spoke to us about impure thoughts, and I never daydreamed then. I listened, because I had them.

"What is the ninth commandment of God?"

"The ninth commandment of God is: Thou shalt not covet thy neighbor's wife, Sister."

"What are we commanded by the ninth commandment?"

"By the ninth commandment, we are commanded to be pure in thought and in desire, Sister."

"What is forbidden by the ninth commandment?"

"The ninth commandment, Sister, forbids all thoughts and desires contrary to chastity."

"Who would want used meat, children?" Sister made a bad-smell face.

I thought about that for a long time. I thought of my mother's meatloaf, and I thought of naked ladies, but I couldn't make the connection. I understood what impure thoughts were. I had them all the time.

For one thing, I knew about kissing, because we played the party game "Truth, Dare, Consequences, Promise, or Repeat"; and we kissed on dares and accepted the consequences if we didn't. If I had to kiss a girl for five minutes, we did it in the hallway, so the old people sitting at their windows across the street wouldn't see us. I knew what I was doing. She did, too.

I never played strip poker, because Donna and the other girls on the block wouldn't play, but I thought about that a lot. Since my mother was the only mother who worked all day, we'd have somewhere to play. And I liked looking at the naked native ladies in *National Geographic* magazines, and I couldn't stop looking.

I learned that I had dirty thoughts, because Adam and Eve ate the apple and were kicked out of the Garden of Eden. Now we were all born with original sin and needed the sacrament of Baptism to be saved.

"But on account of Adam and Eve, we all have the tendency to sin." Sister made a sad face.

Then she'd pause, smile, fold her hands at her chest, and say, "Except the Blessed Virgin Mary, of course."

Well, that was fair. She was Jesus' mother. But those natives and I were still sinners—because of original sin—and Adam and Eve had sinned even before there was an original sin. We never had a chance.

But I never had dirty thoughts about Bonnie. She always wore the school's blue uniform in my daydreams and lying-on-my-bed dreams. And I saw only her face, because my eyes never moved from hers. Even running around the bases, I watched her eyes watching me. I never imagined playing strip poker with Bonnie or Lia. I had butterflies, not dirty thoughts.

I knew that impure thoughts would send me to hell. Eve had disobeyed God, too, but Catholic school girls probably didn't sin that way. Did public school girls have impure thoughts? The nuns told us we were better than the public school kids on 74th Street, but I never believed that.

Some of the boys in my class were not good kids, and all my friends on the block were, and they all went to public school. Where would Adam and Eve go to school? I thought about that but never asked Sister.

Walter, my good friend who lived in the next building, went to P.S. 88 around the corner on Second Avenue, and he was probably smarter than anyone in my class. Except Daniel. Donna went there, too, and she was just as nice as Bonnie.

I knew Walter had dirty thoughts, because some of those *National Geographic* magazines with the naked native ladies belonged to his father.

Would the girls on our block look at those pictures? Would they want to? I wanted to know. They'd listen to a dirty joke and turn away after the punch line. They'd put their hands in front of their faces and laugh but never tell that kind of joke.

Girls were different. That was for sure. During eight years of grammar school, I saw only one girl get hit. Why did Sister hit Helen? I didn't see her do anything. We usually knew the reason for our getting hit.

"Did you throw that, Jamie?"

"No, Sister."

Whack!

I had thrown it.

The Summer of '59

Every summer morning was a school day at three o'clock, the night before a day at Rockaway Beach, or the morning of Christmas Eve. I pulled the door shut, ran to the staircase, and never walked down the stairs. And my hand never touched the banister. I jumped over every other step, and like a gymnast, landed at the bottom on both feet. If a neighbor getting the mail was startled, I'd apologize.

"Sorry, Miss Bergson."

Miss Bergson taught English in an exclusive private school on the West Side. She was a tall, dignified woman with silver hair down to her shoulders. She lived with her mother on my floor. Every year, she bought an entire book of school raffle tickets from me. One chance cost a dime, three for a quarter, and the book for a dollar. Each student had to sell five books for the Catholic missions around the world. I sold all my books to the neighbors.

"That's all right, Jamie. That will be my exercise for the day, but I'm with you in spirit." She was off for the summer, too.

"My friends are waiting for me."

"Well, that is important. Say hello to the boys." I wasn't sure if she was kidding. Miss Bergson didn't know any of my friends.

"Okay . . . Goodbye, Miss Bergson."

Beyond the front door of the building was freedom. There were no parents or nuns out there. The block was ours. We were kids, but there were rules for everything. Our rules. In 1959, some of us drank Mission Grape or Mission Orange soda, and some of us drank Coke or Pepsi, and we were loyal. One of us drank Mission Cream Soda, because nobody ever wanted a slug or even a sip of cream soda—unless it was a very hot day. Archie was cheap.

There was a difference between a sip and a slug when you were sharing. If there were too many boys, you gave only sips. The lips couldn't surround the rim; the top lip had to be inside. On those very hot days, you'd hold your bottle to make sure a lip didn't slip out into a slug. If you saw a slug coming, you pulled the bottle down and away.

"I said a sip!"

There was never an argument. There were rules. A sip was not a slug, and there were witnesses.

Up the street, the guys were sitting on car fenders, ash cans, and Charlie's stoop. Charlie's mother was the janitor and let us sit there every day and night. And as long as we didn't make noise or crush our cigarettes on the steps, she'd also let us sit inside the hallway on very hot and cold days.

After Charlie had shoveled out the furnace during the winter, we helped him carry the cans of ashes up the stairs to the street; and his mother appreciated that. Charlie's father had had a heart attack and died three years ago. The cans were heavy, but they were great to sit on. You couldn't tip over an ash can.

On those days in Charlie's hallway, we drank our sodas, made lists, and argued:

Best centerfielder? Mantle, Mays, or Snider.
Sneakers? Keds or Converse.
Best candy bar? Mars Bar, Milky Way, or Baby Ruth.
Movie? *The Mummy, Ben-Hur*, or *Some Like It Hot*.
Cool actor? Steve McQueen or Clint Eastwood.
Elvis song? "All Shook Up" or "Jailhouse Rock."
Song? "There Goes My Baby" or "A Teenager in Love."
Group? Drifters, Coasters, or Dion and the Belmonts.
Piano player? Little Richard or Jerry Lee Lewis.
Television show? "Wanted: Dead or Alive" or "Rawhide."
Worst soda? Cream.

The morning was cool for the summer, a perfect day for a game of off-the-point. We followed the rules handed down from the older kids on the street. As little kids, we watched them play and learned; and when they were resting, we played. Now they were in high school and had summer jobs. Those who quit school had real jobs. Sandy Thomas was even getting married.

The big kids didn't come around much anymore, so we were the big kids now. Two of my friends even dropped out of junior high school and got good delivery jobs at the A&P. In September, some of us would be starting high school, but nothing was ever going to change. We were best friends for life, and that was more important than anything.

All summer long, every day, all day, we played off-the-point. We played near the corner drug store at the "johnny pump," the fire hydrant, so a parked Chevy or Ford wouldn't block the game. Two boys on a team. One in the street for grounders and line drives. One on the sidewalk behind him for fly balls.

From the candy store for a quarter, we bought a "Spaldeen," which passed "the test" when it bounced up to our belts dropped from our foreheads. Lowell, the candy store man, complained that we were getting his balls dirty. We'd wait for him to say that and laugh. Lowell also made great egg creams.

We threw the ball down at the base molding of the wall. Not like the kids across the avenue where they played stoop ball. We had the better game. If they didn't hit the point of the step, the ball bounced to the infielder or shot straight up and hit the bottom of the fire escape above it. Not us. If we missed the point, the ball hit the wall above or below the point, and it bounced into the street.

One bounce, a single.

Two bounces, a double.

Three bounces, a triple.

Sometimes we argued about that, too.

"Single!"

"It bounced twice!"

"No, it didn't!"

"Don't cheat, Ronnie!"

"Put your glasses on, Charlie!"

"I don't need glasses!"

"You do when you see double!"

When the ball hit the point, it made a clean sound like an echo and bounced off the building across the street for a home run—unless it was caught off the wall. Then it was an out. If it got stuck on the fire escape, we boosted someone, usually me because I was light, up to the ladder to get it—unless there was a dog. If the ball hit a window, we ran.

Once, we broke a window. We came back and chipped in for a new one. If we wanted to play there again, we had no choice.

When the boys greeted me in the morning, it felt good. I was one of the 75th Street guys. Most of us were skinny and short, and wore white t-shirts, dungarees, and sneakers. Except Daniel. He always wore chinos and shirts with collars. If you didn't know Daniel, you'd think he lifted weights. But he never had. He was born with muscles.

When Butchie wore short pants on the first hot day, we pointed and laughed, and Archie screamed,

"Somebody, get a Brownie and take a picture quick! Look at those plump knees! Put them together, and they look like your mama's beee-hind."

We never wore short pants; girls wore "shorts." Butchie surprised us, but he didn't care and wore them all summer.

"Hey, Marilyn . . . Butchie, I mean."

Butchie had light blond hair and an answer for everything.

"You wish you had these knees, Archi*balls*."

Archie hated to be called Archiballs and lit a cigarette. After a while Archie stopped kidding Butchie, but we never wore "Butchie pants."

We were all about the same age, thirteen and fourteen. Butchie was the youngest and a terrific singer. I was the second youngest, and the shortest, but the fastest runner. I was thirteen and nine months. I'd be fourteen in November. Daniel was thirteen and ten months, and the best all-around athlete. Charlie just turned fourteen and could make anything out of wood and leather. Ronnie was also fourteen and had a real girlfriend.

Archie was the oldest. He just turned fifteen, and we used to say he slept on his bike. He lived down on Third Avenue

63

near the 59th Street Bridge and rode his English racer back and forth every day. He could do a wheelie and then stand on the seat. Archie could've been in the circus.

Archie never played ball, though. He made errors look good, and it took us awhile to realize he couldn't play. We were serious about our games. No one ever picked Archie for his side, but Archie didn't care. Sometimes, he'd ride his bike in front of us to stop a game. When Daniel hit him in the back with his fastball, Archie stopped fooling around. Daniel had a great arm.

Ronnie was a very good player, too, but he rarely played. He was in love with Cookie, who was the sweetest girl on the block.

"Leave Butchie alone, Archie. I like his short pants."

"You girls really stick together, Cookie."

"Hushabye, Hushabye, oh, poor Archie, don't you cry," sang Butchie. I think he knew the lyrics of every song on the radio, and 1959 was the summer of the Mystics.

Ronnie and Cookie met in the fifth grade and started "going steady" the second day of school. When Ronnie saw her walk around the corner, he'd lob the ball to one of us, wipe his hands on his pants down to his knees, and open his arms wide.

"Here comes my honey . . . my sweetie . . . my beautiful wife!"

Running his fingers through his wavy hair and taking long bow-legged strides, he'd walk up to Cookie. She'd smile and kiss him, then smile and wave to us; and hand in hand, they'd turn, wave, and disappear around the corner. We wouldn't see Ronnie for the rest of the day.

Since we spoke so much about girls and having sex with them, I wondered about Ronnie and Cookie. I never asked. No one did. Ronnie would never tell—and probably would kill someone. That made sense to me. If you loved the girl, you respected her. You didn't touch her. But if she let you, you never told anyone. If you didn't love her, well, that was different.

"Yah, she let me feel . . ."

Central Park was our playground, our place in the country. We always walked up 72nd Street, and if the Schraffts's curtain was open, we'd stop and make hungry faces at the people eating lunch. On Park Avenue, we'd look south at the New York Central Building at Grand Central. Once inside the park, we'd pass the small Mother Goose playground and then pretend we were tap dancers in the bandshell near Sheep's Meadow, where we played tackle in the winter and hardball in the summer. One year, we even had a coach.

Pat Brady was our cop-on-the-beat. If the older boys were drinking beer from cans in paper bags, he'd walk up to them.

"Hey, guys. If you're not sitting on barstools, say goodbye."

"Goodbye, Pat." The boys would quickly get off the stoop and leave.

If we were making too much noise singing "Stagger Lee" with Lloyd Price on the radio, Pat would make a face.

"You guys make me stagger."

Usually just seeing Pat would stop our singing. Then he'd talk to us about smoking and cancer.

"You're killing yourselves with those coffin nails."

Since our parents worked on weekends—or rested after a long, hard week—we never saw them at our games. And that was the way we liked it. Total freedom. We were used to organizing teams and booking games with other teams on the meadow for the following week. But when Pat volunteered to be our baseball and football coach, we said yes immediately, because we liked him so much.

We never had a coach before. He'd meet us in the park every Saturday morning and run plays in practice—and sometimes umpire or ref the games. One Saturday morning in the winter, Pat couldn't believe his eyes.

"Where are your shoes, Ronnie?"

"Under that tree, Pat."

"Why?"

"Mass."

"Yeah?"

"They're my Sunday shoes."

"What about your Sunday pants?"

"I can't take them off, right?"

"Stop laughing and put your shoes on, Ronnie. Some of those guys are wearing spikes."

"But my mother will kill me."

"And your pants? She'll kill you anyway. But those guys will put holes in your feet. Maybe you shouldn't play today." Ronnie quickly ran to his shoes.

We weren't very good, but we had a great time. The meadow wasn't a Little League field or high school gridiron. It was a large grassland with more dirt than grass, surrounded by trees, and beyond and above them, the city skyscrapers. There were no bases, so we used cardboard or our shirts, and there were always several games going on at once.

When I played shortstop or second, I'd have another game's outfielder behind me. When someone yelled "Heads-up!" we all looked down and covered our heads with gloves. That happened most innings. It was a normal part of the game. Once the ball was fielded, we continued our game.

After a long game on a hot day, we stood on long lines of sweaty kids for the two water fountains near the meadow and talked up the old story that someone had put a worm in the spout.

"Any worm yet? Last week, a kid choked on a long one. You could see the end of it wiggle on his chin."

I never saw anyone leave the line.

After every loss—and we lost baseball games all the time—Pat took us to an ice cream parlor and treated all of us. Then, using his notes, he'd go over the game. He'd explain what each of us did wrong—and, more important, right.

"You guys are getting better. Teamwork is your strength." We would have done anything for Pat.

Somehow, one Sunday morning, we won a game; but walking back down 72nd Street, we argued about missed chances and poor plays.

"Me! You threw it in the dirt!"

"You didn't stretch."

"I liked you guys better when you lost," Pat added.

He didn't take us to the ice cream parlor that day; and a month later, when he hurt his back on the job, he stopped being our coach and our cop-on-the-beat. We never saw Pat again, but we continued picking up games in the park.

When the August temperature hit 97 degrees, we didn't feel like going to the park, and we didn't feel like playing punchball or off-the-point. To Butchie, the street smelled of "garbage and doggie dunggie." I never heard Butchie curse. We weren't Butchie. We had a lot of good names for it. We sat in the hallway and shared Daniel's Mission Grape. On those hot days, we didn't argue much.

If we were still thirsty, and no one had a dime, we went to the saloon down the street or to the barbershop, where Pinky the barber let us fill our soda bottle from the sink. Our parents said he was a bookie. Maybe he was, since he was a terrible barber. But he was a good guy. Then we'd go back to Charlie's building for the afternoon.

For two whole days during a late summer heat wave, I didn't go out, a first in thirteen summers. My friends rang my bell and called up to my window, but I shook my head and raised *Gone with the Wind* to the glass. Confused, they waved me off and walked away. But there was another reason I was staying home. My mother had bought our first air conditioner.

Before we had air conditioning, sleeping was awful. Looking for a dry spot, I rolled back and forth on the sheet and flipped the damp pillow over and over. By morning, I ended up against the wall where I had found a fresh fan breeze. But the heat wasn't the only problem. I couldn't ignore the buzzing, because mosquitoes loved me.

In the middle of the night, my mother would close the Venetian blinds to prevent reinforcements and open the lights, and we'd throw small cushions against the ceiling to squash them. By the end of the summer, the ceiling was a mosquito graveyard marked by tiny splotches of blood.

Now those sweaty nights were gone. I was going to enjoy the cool air—and Rhett and Scarlett. I was thirteen and I was in love with love.

I also had a crush on one of the girls who had started to hang out with us. Daniel met Cindy at a parish dance in June. Every night she met him on the block, and she brought her friends and a radio. There were other girls on our street, but they were always there. These girls were exciting; they lived uptown on 84th Street.

When they danced with one another—and they were always dancing—I knew I was in love with Sherri, spelled with an "i." She had long brown hair and dark eyes. She was going into the eighth grade and had a good figure. When Sherri and Cindy danced together, Sherri always looked at me and smiled. I liked her eyes and her cute figure; but most important, I liked feeling the butterflies in my chest again. When I heard the Flamingos sing "I Only Have Eyes for You" on Cindy's radio, I watched Sherri dance.

Labor Day was a week away. I was excited about going to high school. I never liked grammar school, and for the first time in eight years, I'd have men teaching me. That would be a nice change from eight years of nuns. I was also getting tired of the hot weather—even with the air conditioner.

I knew our days of playing off-the-point were coming to an end. The building across the street was boarded up for demolition. Soon, a home run ball would be a lost ball among broken bricks, wood, and glass; and next year, people in the new building would probably call the police if a ball hit their windows. It was going to be a doorman building. The block was changing. All the blocks were.

A few buildings down the street were also boarded up, and old neighborhood friends had already moved to Queens and Long Island. When I was younger, we all played Simon Says and Ringolevio. We also played Truth, Dare, Consequences, Promise, or Repeat. We were little kids, but we knew a lot about making out for a dare—and which building hallways were good for being daring.

Before my mother bought our television set, I spent many afternoons in Walter's apartment next door. He was my first friend on the block, and the first kid on the block to have a TV. Suddenly Walter was very popular. He had a television set before he even had a refrigerator. His mother used the icebox in the summer and the fire escape in the winter for the meat, milk, and vegetables.

Upstairs in his building, Daniel, Walter, and I would knock on Philly's door at eight o'clock at night, because we knew his sister Eileen was taking a bath in the kitchen bathtub. Eileen was sixteen and looked great in sweaters. She could have been a pin-up girl or movie star as far as we were concerned.

"Is Philly home?" we'd call through the door.

"Mom! Tell them to go away!"

"What? We can't hear you, Philly! Did you say to come in? Okay, Philly, we're coming in!"

"Mom! Is the door shut? Philly's friends are trying to come in!"

When we heard Eileen's mother's voice in the kitchen, we ran down the stairs and out of the building in case her father was home, too.

Now Walter, Philly, and Eileen were gone. Many friends were gone.

Early one Sunday morning when the workmen were off, Charlie, Archie, Butchie, Daniel, and I ripped the plywood off a window in the backyard with Charlie's crowbar and climbed in. We were looking for linoleum to use for "ammo guns," which were two pieces of wood nailed together to look like a gun with a nail at the end of the barrel. Then we stretched a rubber band back to a notch carved out at the other end.

Once we stuck the small square of linoleum between the two strands of the rubber band and released it at the notch, we could shoot the piece of ammo across the street. Ammo wars were very popular on our block and less dangerous than shooting peas or paper clips with rubber bands, which could take "an eye out."

There was a lot of light in the hallway, because all the windows and doors on the upper floors were removed; but we had to watch where we walked. Most of the flooring was also gone. The workman had laid wide boards running to all the apartments and stairs. We knew there were rats in the building, because we'd see them at night on the sidewalk when the workmen left. We made sure to make a lot of noise.

"You can look but you better not touch." Butchie loved the Coasters.

"Poison iv-y-y-y-y, Poison iv-y-y-y-y."

The stairs were still there, but the banisters were gone. We walked up to the second floor and looked into Walter's apartment. Nothing was left. In the backyard, we had seen the oak iceboxes that were thrown out of the windows. Probably too heavy to carry down the stairs. And who would want them anyway?

Even the pipes in the kitchen had been ripped out of the walls. But I knew this was Walter's apartment. Walter and I had watched his mother and father hang the wallpaper of flowers in the living room and argue.

"I told you it was harder than you think." That was Walter's father. But it looked good to me. I liked the color of the flowers, because they reminded me of Walter's mother. Even though his father was always angry about something or someone, she always smiled when we were around. Walter told us that a bee had stung her tongue a long time ago, so she rarely opened her mouth to speak. When I heard that, I liked her even more.

We walked up to Philly's apartment, and Butchie sang, "He's a clown, that Archie Brown." Butchie really loved the Coasters.

"Charlie Brown, you dope."

"I know Archi*balls*."

"Shut up, Marilyn."

Philly's apartment looked like Walter's. Empty.

"The tub was right here. This wall watched Eileen take a bath every night, Jamie. I'm taking a piece home." Archie chipped a piece of plaster with his hammer.

"And she dried herself on this linoleum."

Under the linoleum, we found newspapers dating back to 1910. Newspapers were a good way to keep the rooms warmer in the winter. Only the kitchen had pipes—and heat—and everyone sat in there. Philly's television set was on top of the refrigerator. But even in the summer, we all sat in the kitchen.

Looking for more newspapers, we ripped up all the linoleum. Under the last layer, we found a concrete platform near the outside wall.

"Look at this. There was a coal stove here."

"Walter and Philly never had a coal stove."

"I guess the people in 1910 did."

The four apartments on each floor shared a bathroom in the hall. In the 4th floor hall bathroom, Archie found false teeth in the medicine cabinet. Somehow he made them snap at Butchie, and we all laughed.

"Gross!"

"Skeeve! Hey, Archie. Tell your mother we found them."

"Hey, that's funny, Marilyn. But I think these pearls will look great under your blond hair. Put them in and give us a smile, or I'll bite those juicy knees of yours with them."

"You can look but you better not touch, Archie . . . *balls*!" sang Butchie as he ran down the stairs.

"I guess it's a bite then."

Archie chased Butchie, and Daniel and Charlie ran down the stairs after them.

Walking slowly, I looked into all the apartments on each landing and stopped on the second floor, and sat on Walter's windowsill for a while to look at his mother's wallpaper.

Daniel Fitzpatrick

Daniel was the coolest kid in the first grade. After a sweaty game of tag or sword fighting in the schoolyard, his straight dark hair framed his face like a horseshoe; but he always returned to class with hair parted and shirt tucked in. Daniel carried a comb in his back pocket. More important, he was smart and kind. He was as smart as any girl, and he never made fun of anyone's buckteeth or parents who spoke with a foreign accent. He became my first friend in the first grade at St. Jude's, because he spoke to me.

"I'm Daniel."

"I'm James. Jamie."

"I'm Daniel. Daniel."

"Daniel-Daniel?"

"No, just Daniel."

We didn't always understand each other; but he was patient, and we soon became best friends.

You could never call him Danny, Dan, or Fitz. If you did, he ignored you. You had to call him Daniel or Fitzpatrick. Since most of us had nicknames and wanted to call him Danny, we tried to change his mind. In the schoolyard one day, we all yelled "Danny! Danny!" as loud as we could on the count of three, but he kept walking without looking back.

Then we all yelled "Dan" and held the "n" for a long time to fool him, but that didn't work, either. He watched a pigeon—or an invisible airplane—do figure eights in the sky. Then, with outstretched arms, he tight-roped a crooked crack in the sidewalk and was near the schoolyard gate.

As soon we all yelled "Daniel! Daniel, come back!" he stopped. With his arms still out, he made a wide airplane turn, smiled, and walked a straight line back to us. Most of us laughed, and he laughed, but some of the other boys didn't like it.

"All Daniels are Danny. Everyone knows that. What is he? Stuck-up or what? Dannn . . . yeelll," they whined.

But Daniel was unpredictable and funny, and soon everyone liked him, and everyone called him Daniel. During religion classes, no one ever mentioned that he was half Jewish.

Years later, while we waited for the second game of a doubleheader to begin, I told Daniel about my father's abducting me when I was very young and my jumping into a getaway car with my mother and her friends; and he told me about his parents' uncommon marriage after the war and his father's reason for sending him to a Catholic school.

Daniel called himself "Jewrish, the only one in school." Dottie, his mother, was Russian-Jewish; and John, his father, was Irish-Catholic, but they were born here in the city. They met at the brewery, where they both worked after the war, and married against the wishes of their parents, friends, family priest and rabbi, and even some neighbors.

Neither of them was religious, but Daniel was baptized a Catholic, so he could attend St. Jude's later on. The nuns were good to John's mother when his father had deserted them. Dottie wasn't religious either, so being baptized and going to St. Jude's were fine with her—so long as no one picked on Daniel for being half Jewish. She preferred his going to a public school.

"Dottie, you don't want him with those people in that public school on First Avenue near the bridge. They're tough kids."

"But the public school is only a few blocks away from St. Jude's. Why are they tough there, John?"

"They're mostly Italians with maybe a Czech and a Jew thrown in. Who knows? The Czechs have their own Catholic school over there on First Avenue. The Germans and Hungarians are uptown. But our public school is in the middle of an Italian neighborhood, so it makes sense that most of the kids are Italians. St. Jude is in an Irish neighborhood and almost all the kids are Irish. He'll be with his own."

"His own? There'll be no Jews at St. Jude's. I'm not sure I like that, and I'd rather he know a lot of different kids. Italians, Czechs, Polish—and especially other Jewish kids—would be nice. And a lot of people don't like Jews, John. Remember?"

John's mother wanted an Irish daughter-in-law, "or—at least—a Catholic one." Dottie's parents wanted a Jewish son-in-law. They lost so many family members in Europe, they wanted Jewish babies. But when Daniel was born, he became theirs; and for him, they celebrated all the holidays together. He was Jewrish.

"He'll meet all those other kids soon enough, Dottie. I work with some of their fathers at the brewery."

"What are they like?"

"Nice guys."

At work, John was a popular man, a Pepsi man—"unless you put a gun to his head in the Sahara Desert and gave him a Coke."

That was the running joke among his co-workers, who were all beer men. They'd invite John for a drink on payday, but John was also a family man, who celebrated Friday at home with a Pepsi and pizza. I never saw John drunk or mean. When I read about Atticus, the father in *To Kill a Mockingbird*, I thought of John. He was the best father in the neighborhood.

"So what's wrong with their kids, John?"

"Nothing, but people stick together. He'd be the outsider."

"We're married."

"Come on, Dottie. You know that was different. You couldn't help yourself." John moved toward Dottie.

"Not so much right now." Dottie stepped back. "I don't want them to be physically attracted to Daniel. I want them to be nice to him."

"They will be. His name is Daniel Fitzpatrick, and he looks like me. No one's going to give him a hard time about being half Jewish at St. Jude's."

"Daniel's not half a boy. I don't want him hiding behind his father's name and face. He's half Irish—and half Jewish."

"Dottie, you're not going to find many Jewish kids in that public school, either. There just aren't many Jews in the neighborhood. You'd need to go to the Lower East Side to find a public school with lots of them."

"He'll go to your school, but I'll be watching."

Every evening around the kitchen table, Daniel described his day and our jokes about Sister Lampshade or Father Tulips, but he never mentioned the lessons about the "Pharisees who forced Pontius Pilate to crucify Jesus Christ, our Lord and Savior."

I sat two rows over and one seat back from Daniel, and I'd watch him when the sisters taught that Jesus died for our sins and rose from the dead on Easter Sunday. With folded hands on top of his desk, he'd sit very still and stare at them.

We were both half something else. During world history lessons in the 4th grade, I hated to hear about the French losing another battle or war to the English or Germans, or about America saving France again. I was half French, but all of me took it personally.

When I'd mention that to Daniel, he'd remind me that Lafayette and France helped us during our revolution against England. I knew that, because it was in our history book, but Daniel's saying it always worked. He wanted me to feel better about myself, and I did.

But this was much worse. When Sister mentioned the crucifixion and the Pharisees, I remembered my father's army pictures of the dead concentration people stacked one on top of the other. I thought of Daniel's mother and my neighbor Miss Bergson. After class on the line to lunch, I'd poke him in the ribs and say, "Jesus was a Jew, Daniel." Of course, he knew that. He never smiled, but it made me feel better to say it.

Daniel lived around the corner from me on 74th Street and was one of the 75th Street guys. We always played on the same punch-ball and touch-football teams, and we usually won, because he was so athletic. Daniel had a great arm, and he could throw a runner out from two manhole covers away.

But we always took opposite sides of an argument. He never lost his temper. I did and lost arguments. Sometimes we'd argue about Yogi and Campy. Or who was the better short stop? Scooter or Pee Wee. Daniel was a Yankee fan, and I was a Brooklyn Dodger fan, the only one in Manhattan as far as I knew. After the Dodgers won the World Series by beating the Yankees in seven games, Daniel asked, "How many games did Mantle miss, Jamie?"

Daniel hated to lose.

"Face it, Jamie. The Dodgers only won, because *the Mick* was injured. Well, at least, they won *one* World Series."

Yankee fans hated to lose.

When the Dodgers left Brooklyn for Los Angeles, I went with Daniel to Yankee Stadium on weekends. After watching games on black-and-white television, I was never prepared for the brilliant green field and blue sky in front of me. I felt the same way about hearing and smelling the ocean at Rockaway Beach or seeing Manhattan from the windy observation deck of the Empire State Building. I was never prepared.

We'd sit in right field for batting practice. We never caught any balls, but it was fun chasing them in the aisles; and once in a while, Yankee right fielder Hank Bauer, a favorite of ours, would flip balls back to the kids who weren't lucky. Daniel was lucky once with a Bauer ball.

One year, Daniel just missed catching Ted Williams's last home run at Yankee Stadium. His picture appeared in the *Sunday Times Sports Section*, because he sat near the man who had caught it. I didn't go that day. Daniel's mother bought three papers. One for her mother and father, one for John's mother, and one for her living room wall.

Of course, I'd root for the visiting team. I'd cheer for Ted Williams and Rocky Colavito, Luis Aparicio and Jimmy Piersall. They weren't the Brooklyn Dodgers, but they were all I had, and they were fun to watch.

We'd bring sandwiches and bags of peanuts, and watch double headers; and before the second game began, we'd sneak down to the box seats on the field. Sometimes the ushers left us alone, and sitting on the wooden seats for five hours was never a problem. We could see the ballplayers' faces when they swung their bats and ran to first.

I was a Yankee hater. I had to be. They beat the Dodgers in the World Series year after year. Moose Skowron wasn't Gil Hodges, and Yogi Berra wasn't Roy Campanella, but they were also fun to watch. When Yogi hit a long home run into the stands, Daniel would turn to me and smile. What could I say? A home run is a home run. It was exciting.

After every game, we ran with all the fans onto the field, the very field we saw on television, the field where major leaguers caught grounders and fly balls. After yelling and running here and there for a while, we walked past the Babe Ruth and Lou Gehrig monuments out the gate to the subway. There was no better way to spend a Sunday in the city, even for an *old* Brooklyn Dodger fan.

Before Daniel had a job and money to buy cigarettes, he'd follow a grownup in the street and imitate the way he walked and smoked. With his two fingers up in the air, he'd bring the imaginary cigarette to his mouth and blow out imaginary smoke. Sometimes he'd fake a cough and pat his chest, and we'd laugh. When the smoker threw his away, Daniel would pick up the "dincher," kiss-it-up-to-God for good hygiene, and we'd sit on a nearby stoop to pass it around.

We were eleven, but we were Humphrey Bogart in *The Maltese Falcon.* If we had two cents, we'd buy a "loosie" from a candy store on 74th that sold to kids. But when Daniel had a job, he'd let me grub Luckies from him all day. Daniel always had some kind of delivery job, and he was very generous. Of course, I'd promise to pay him back.

The days he didn't work, Daniel and I picked up jobs in the neighborhood. As a team, we washed windows. Most of the tenements on the block had rotten window frames, because they were so old. The glass rattled even when we just opened the window.

I would do the outside glass, pressing my heels against the wall below the window for balance. Daniel would hold my belt, so both my hands would be free to spray and wipe. Once I was done, he would pull me in and do the inside himself. Sometimes I'd have to go out again to get the spots I had missed. When we got bored, we joked.

"All right, Lachlan, give me a buck three eighty, you piker you."

"Don't make me laugh, Fitzpatrick."

"Laugh? Who's joking? Pay or flap those skinny arms."

For the next window, he'd go out and I'd hold his belt.

"Give me all your cigarettes, Fitzpatrick, or you smoked your last one a minute ago." Since Daniel always wore a shirt with a pocket, I saw his full pack.

"No way. They'll break my fall."

He hated to lose.

After lunch we'd go to construction sites where workers gave us their empty beer and soda bottles for deposit.

"Here you go, kid. Buy your girlfriend a flower." A box of quart bottles at a nickel apiece would buy a bouquet.

One bottle, a Mars bar.

Two bottles, a Mission Grape soda.

Six bottles, a movie ticket or a pack of cigarettes.

Twenty bottles, a 45 rpm record of "Mack the Knife."

And the work was safer than washing windows.

If I was desperate to go to a movie and couldn't find a way to make thirty cents, I'd go to the butcher shop on York Avenue and mix hamburger meat with blood and fat. That was my least favorite way of making money, because my hands would get cold—and smell awful. I never told my mother, because she'd forbid me to go there again, and she bought our meat at a different butcher anyway. But she was cautious and always watched him grind the meat.

I don't think Daniel was afraid of anything. When we were eleven, my mother was taking us to Rockaway Beach one Saturday. We were standing on the platform, watching the small train light get larger and larger, when I heard an echo of a crash and my mother's scream. I looked at her, and she screamed, "Daniel! Daniel!" I turned to look at Daniel, but he wasn't next to me. I looked down.

While Daniel was standing below on the tracks, he placed our water cooler at our feet; and before we had a chance to scream "Train!" he was back up on the platform. When the train came into the station, and Daniel saw my mother covering her face with her hands, he spent the next ten minutes apologizing to her. Rubbing his hands together, he didn't stop speaking. I never saw him so nervous. And we didn't get on that train or the next one, because my mother sat on the bench behind her.

"But the train light was so far away. I had plenty of time. It was all the way in the tunnel. The light was so small." He kept speaking. He liked my mother very much and felt terrible that he had frightened her. "I'm sorry. I dropped it and had to . . ."

"Never, never do anything like that again, Daniel. Never, Daniel. If your poor mother . . . the poor thing."

My mother was so angry that she chose a seat across from us, opened her book, didn't turn the page for a long time, and never looked up. When we finally got to the beach, she was speaking again.

"All right, boys, let's try to have a nice day. I really need it now. Who wants a sandwich? Salami or turkey?"

"We're going swimming first, Mom. Waves look great."

"Be careful. Follow the rules, boys."

"Sure, Mom."

My mother never saw us swim beyond the buoys or heard the lifeguard blowing his whistle for us to swim in.

"Good waves, boys?

"Great."

"Now, sit down and have a nice sandwich."

I also never told my mother about horseback riding in Central Park. One morning, saving ourselves fifteen cents each, Daniel and I "hitched" a ride on the back of the 86th Street cross-town bus to a stable on the West Side and rented horses for five dollars apiece. For one whole hour. But that was a hundred nickel-beer bottles for one of us alone.

We didn't know what a horn or pommel was, or that there were western and English saddles. But we had seen hundreds of cowboy movies, so we would know how to ride the wildest horses, bareback even. It took us awhile getting up onto the saddles, which were above our heads. We needed to use the unfriendly stable man's stool.

Singing "I'm an old cowhand" and "Keep them doggies rollin' Rawhide!" on the way to Central Park, we were Texas Rangers. And when we were gunslingers, we drew make-believe Colt .45s from make-believe holsters and fired away at anything that moved. We were dangerous hombres. Sometimes we'd even square off against each other and draw our guns. Steve McQueen and Clint Eastwood shoot it out in Central Park.

Back on the block, things we liked were "cool," and cooler things were "boss"—but really boss things were "bo-cool." Steve and Clint were bo-cool. We were only thirteen but bo-cool, too, because we were riding horses in the street with cabs and buses around us. In the park, we galloped and raced each other. Later we'd have stories for the guys who didn't know a thing about horses.

"The horseshoes were louder than the car horns," one of us would say.

"And we could see into the bus windows," the other would say.

The park looked beautiful and peaceful from my saddle. I was ten feet tall and proud. I knew my horse; and he knew it, because I was born to ride. When my horse shook his large head, I patted his powerful dark neck.

"Good boy, Shadow." We had a bond. In the wilds of Central Park, we depended on each other. I could see that Daniel and his horse had the same bond.

When we were about to pass an exit from the path, our horses turned right to leave. We pulled the reins left. With their heads facing left, both horses snorted and made a sharp right out of the park. An hour was an hour, and lunch was four blocks away. They were going home, and they were in a hurry. These horses could tell time.

They ignored our shouts of "Whoa!" and "Easy, fella!" They also ignored the red lights and the moving cars and buses. After hearing the screeching brakes, blaring horns, and determined hoofs striking cobblestones, we gave up.

We grabbed the front of the hornless saddles, lowered our heads, and galloped through the busy West Side streets of New York City. Once the horses were on "their" street, they slowed to a victory trot.

Hunched over and humiliated, we rode into the stable. We weren't Steve McQueen and Clint Eastwood. We weren't even Gabby Hayes and the Cisco Kid's sidekick. But all wasn't lost. At least, we'd have a story to tell the guys later tonight.

"Yeah, it was so cool making all those cars stop . . . and I almost fell off . . . on a cab," Daniel said. "Yeah, a cab!"

"No, we weren't afraid," I said. "It was bo-cool."

We never rode horses again. We stuck to bouncing up and down on the back of buses up Third Avenue and down Lexington Avenue. A bus was predictable.

We had an easier time with Central Park rowboats. When several of us rented boats—and rowed around the bend and out of sight of the boathouse—we were pirates. We splashed one another with the oars, and after crashing into one another's boat a few times, we'd board for the booty.

But when Daniel and I were alone, we'd just float along and practice blowing smoke rings through smoke rings with cigarettes from Daniel's ashtray at home. His parents smoked Winstons.

". . . tastes good *like* a cigarette should."

We emphasized the "like," because Sister had told us over and over it was a "terrible slogan. Awful, awful grammar."

". . . tastes good *as* a cigarette should," Sister had said. "Use 'as' for a clause. Use 'like' for a phrase. Now repeat after me."

Smoking our Winstons and floating on the Central Park Lake, Daniel and I enjoyed the good life during that summer of 1959.

"Winston tastes good . . . *like* . . . a cigarette should!"

It was Labor Day night, the end of summer, and tomorrow I wouldn't be walking the three blocks to grammar school. No more blue corduroy pants and clip-on-tie. No more fountain pens. For eight years, I had very low grades in penmanship. I wrote fairly well with ballpoints and pencils, but we had to use fountain pens for eight years. Tomorrow, I'd take a bus to school and buy a monthly bus pass and yellow-and-maroon school jacket.

It was getting dark earlier, so we didn't play ball after supper. We sat on Charlie's stoop and talked about the girls who were home getting ready for school. Everyone agreed Sherri had the best figure. I didn't say anything, because I liked Sherri. I changed the subject to mosquitoes. Archie sat on the seat of his bike. Daniel took out a deck of cards. The girls usually brought the radio, so we had no music. Even Butchie was quiet.

It didn't feel like September, because it was too warm. But the summer nights were over for me. I was determined to be a good student and was looking forward to tomorrow and the brothers at St. Edmund's. No one knew me there—except Brother Shaye. I even had butterflies in my stomach.

Daniel was going to the Bronx High School of Science, one of the best schools in the city. For the first time in eight years, we wouldn't be in the same classroom. He didn't seem excited or nervous, and the other guys were never excited about school. For some reason, Daniel was giving me an extra-hard time about going home early tonight.

"Come on, Jamie. Play just one hand. I'll let you cheat." He stood up and put his arm around my shoulder.

"No. Gotta go, Daniel."

"You're a big boy, Jamie. You're in high school now."

"I need my beauty sleep, Daniel."

"You may never wake up."

Everyone laughed, and I laughed and was about to turn when Daniel punched me in the forehead with his open palm. My neck snapped back, but I didn't feel anything. It didn't hurt, but I realized he had punched me. I grabbed his shoulder and made a fist with my right hand. We'd never had a fist fight.

We'd never even play-wrestled, and Daniel just hit me in t|
forehead.

"What the hell, Fitzpatrick?"

"No, no. I saved your life."

He had tears in his eyes. He had hit me in the head, a
now he was laughing at me; and to my right and left, Arch
Ronnie, Charlie, and Butchie were pointing and laughing
was back in the first grade, back with the bullies, surroundi
me, singing, "All the girls in France do the hula-hula danc
But these boys were my friends. Daniel was my best friend

"That's really funny, you goddamn faggots. And you .
You punch me and laugh, you goddamn Jew."

Daniel stopped laughing and stared at my forehead. Arch
Ronnie, Charlie, and Butchie lowered their arms. No one w
laughing. I hated them.

"Yeah, not so funny now, not so funny now. How does
feel, you faggots?" I turned to leave.

"No, no, wait, Jamie." I stopped, turned, and tighten
both fists. Daniel slowly raised his thumb and index finger
touch my forehead. I leaned back a little and slowly raised r
right fist.

"Please, Jamie. I want to show you something."

When he pulled his hand away, he held a dead horse
between his pinched fingers.

"Look."

He had crushed the biggest horsefly I'd ever seen again
my forehead. It was huge.

"Bring it to school tomorrow for show and tell. Impress tl
brothers and your new friends."

"Jesus, Daniel. I'm sorry."

I couldn't even smile. Never in all our arguments had w
attacked each other's background. That would be attackir
each other's mother.

"Hey, don't be sorry. If you punched me in the head, I'd sa
something pretty awful to you, too, you bigot."

"No, really, Daniel, I'm really sorry. I thought you just wei
nuts and punched me in the goddamn head. Oh, Jesus."

"Forget about it, Lachlan. I'll talk to you tomorrow. Come on, smile."

"Yeah, talk to you tomorrow, Daniel. And thanks for saving my life." I faked a smile and turned to leave.

"You want this monster?" Exaggerating its weight, he held it out to me with both hands.

"No, thanks. Too heavy for me. I'd probably get a hernia." I was missing Daniel tomorrow already.

"But I thought frogs liked flies, Lachlan." The guys laughed, and then I was able to smile. Daniel hated to lose.

"You said that to say what, you bigot? I'm telling my mother, Fitzpatrick."

This time, we all laughed.

Brother and Miss Crabtree, 1959

In September of 1959, I was no longer a big-shot eighth grader. I was now a short high school freshman, who took a city bus and wore a jacket—and a real tie—to school. The night before, my neighbor Dr. Zeeman taught me the Windsor knot. He said I was a natural, because it took me only five times to learn it. No more blue clip-ons or blue corduroy pants for me.

No more mandatory fountain pens or inkwells to be refilled. In high school, we were permitted to use ballpoint pens, which didn't leak and color our fingers inky blue.

No sitting in the front pews with the entire school for nine o'clock mass on Sundays, no standing around the room for spelling bees on Thursdays, and no being taken by the nuns to the free Friday clinic where student dentists never used Novocaine.

No wearing stiff paper costumes, singing, and dancing for all the parents every spring. I never got a lead, because I sang as badly as I danced, and that was fine with me. I didn't have to memorize any lines, and since I was short for my age, no one saw my dancing. Our director, Madame Duvalliere, called it "unique" and put me in the last row, and my mother agreed with her.

No more standing by our desks, reciting answers from blue Baltimore Catechism books:

"Did God abandon man after Adam fell into sin?"

"No, Sister, God did not abandon man after Adam fell into sin."

"Who is the Saviour of all men?"

"The Saviour of all men is Jesus Christ, Sister."

"When was Christ born?"

"Christ was born of the Blessed Virgin Mary on Christmas Day, Sister."

And for the first time in eight years, there were no girls or nuns in the classroom; in fact, there wasn't a woman in the building—if you didn't count the two cafeteria ladies and the principal's secretary, Mrs. Brennan. But Mrs. B. was almost invisible, because she sat behind the high counter in Brother Shaye's office.

But you knew she was there. Just above the counter we could see the tight bun of her white hair keeping time to her whistling—and she was always whistling songs from Broadway shows. Mrs. B. was a good whistler, and since the office was near the school's entrance, we'd hear her while we were entering and leaving the building.

Once for several days, we heard, "I'm Gonna Wash That Man Right Outta My Hair," and joked that she was whistling about Brother.

After eight years of grammar school where we—calling out "Sssssister!" when we knew the answers—sounded like a classroom of snakes, we now had to raise our hands and wait for our teacher to call on us.

"Yes, Lachlan?"

That was a relief, since saying "Brother" was another challenge for an old stutterer like me. Here, there was no competition, and I could take my time.

"B-B-Brother, n-number four is . . ."

But most important, for the first time, I saw men in front of the classroom. There were many men who lived in my building, but they were neighbors. And even if two of them were like grandfathers to me, this was different. These men were my teachers; they were authority figures. I saw them five days a week, and I watched them very closely. As a result, I became a much better student, because I wanted them to like me, and I wanted to be like them.

I met Brother Shaye last June during my interview. Since my grammar school grades were poor, our pastor, Father Quinn, suggested I meet Brother Shaye. Unlike Father "Tulips," his assistant priest in the parish, Father Quinn—and Mother Superior—believed I had potential.

"Brother Shaye and I are old friends, Jamie. Last night, I gave him a call and told him all about you and your background. He wants to meet you, Jamie. Your grades don't reflect your ability. You're a bright boy, but you need direction and guidance. You need to stop your daydreaming. What do you think of that, Jamie?"

"What about Father Tulips . . . Ronan? Sorry, Father."

We boys called Father Ronan, "Tulips," because his lips ballooned when he smiled. No one liked Father Tulips. Everyone liked Father Quinn.

"Father Ronan thinks I should go to a vocational high school."

"What do you think, Jamie?"

"I don't know. I never thought much about it. He's right about me not liking school."

"That's what your mother tells me. But she also says that you like to read. Is that true, Jamie? You like to read?"

"Yes, Father."

"Good. So do I. Tell me when your mother's free, and I'll make the appointment myself."

We had a problem. My mother was never free. She had a new job and was afraid to ask for a day off.

"Not a problem, Jamie. Brother Shaye will see you next Saturday. He and the other brothers live in the building. Ten o'clock. Let me know if that's okay with your mother."

"Thank you, Father."

On hot summer evenings, people sat on stoops and beach chairs, drank soda, and socialized with their neighbors. During the day, old women and men leaned on windowsills, sometimes with their dogs, and watched the theater of our roller skating and playing ball. They were always there, and we were always safe.

"Stop hitting him! Pick on somebody your own size, ya big jerk ya!"

If we were noisy at night, they threw pots of water out the window.

"Hey! Shut up down there! Next time, I'll call the cops on ya!"

We'd scatter and laugh but, ten minutes later, come back and speak softly—until we forgot. Sometimes the water got us, and we cursed.

I found out much later that Brother Shaye and I had a neighborhood connection. His brother had married the daughter of Mrs. Whelan, who lived down the street from me and sat on her beach chair. When I passed her on the street, she always asked, "How's Mama?" She had a kind face and seemed to care.

"She's good, Mrs. Whelan."

She and my mother never really spoke, but when they passed each other on the street, they'd smile and say hello. If you walked up and down the same street every day, you were recognized. We were a friendly block.

Once you turned the corner, you were a stranger. We ten-year-olds knew where to smoke our ashtray-stolen Winstons and Chesterfields. Around the corner on Second or Third Avenue, we showed off with smoke rings. We were cool.

On Saturday morning, my mother and I took the Lexington Avenue bus to St. Edmund's. When I saw the school with the gold letters over the door, I realized that Father Quinn meant business. There it was. My high school if I did well on this interview. Father Quinn and Mother Superior were always looking out for my mother and me.

We got to the building at 9:50, so we waited. Next door, there was a music store playing "Good Golly Miss Molly." I thought Little Richard was cool and bit my lower lip, closed my eyes, and kept the beat with my shoulders and head. My mother made a "do-you-know-where-you-are?" face.

"Stop it, Jamie. If Brother Shaye sees you, he won't open the door."

She looked at her watch again. At ten o'clock, she pushed the door open, but it wouldn't move. We both pushed it. It didn't move.

"Father Quinn said Saturday, right?"

"Yeah."

"Don't say 'Yeah' here, Jamie."

"Yeah." I smiled. She didn't. "Yes."

"Well, let's try this big button." When she pressed it, we heard the bell despite Little Richard.

"From the early, early morning . . ."

It was the loudest bell I had ever heard. It was almost a gong. Within a minute, a man with "dark laughing eyes," my mother's description, opened the large wooden door. Like Father Quinn, he was wearing a collar and black robe. I had never seen a brother, so I was surprised. They looked the same. Why was he called "brother"? My mother thought he looked like a movie star.

"Did you make all that noise?"

"Sorry, Brother, I pressed this . . ."

"No, no, I'm kidding. We need to hear the bell if we're on the top floor."

He saw immediately that we hadn't realized he was kidding us. We were too nervous to kid, so he changed the tone of his voice.

"The music next door doesn't help, does it? Come on in, please. We'll sit in the library."

Following closely behind Brother Shaye, we walked up several steps and made two right turns for the school's small library. When we passed the glass trophy case, I stopped for a moment.

"No, no. Take a look. Do you play any sports?"

"Baseball and football."

"Those teams we don't have. Think basketball, track, or swimming. We have a pool downstairs. This was a YMCA building before us."

"Yes, I will."

I never played basketball, but I could swim and run.

"Please have a seat, so we can get to know one another. Now let me say that it's very nice to meet you, Mrs. Lachlan, and you, Jamie. Thank you for coming."

I liked him right away. I saw that he was being kind to my mother, who was more nervous than I was. He was trying to calm her down. No Catholic school would take me because of my grades—and behavior—in class; and she didn't want to send me to a public school.

A few years ago, she had seen the movie *Blackboard Jungle* and believed that most public high schools were schools for juvenile delinquents. My best friend, Daniel, was going to the Bronx High School of Science. That was a special school for very intelligent students, but Daniel was smarter than I was.

"So, Jamie, Father Quinn tells me you're a big reader. What was the last book you read?"

"*Gone with the Wind.*"

"*Gone with the Wind*! That's a big book for a young man."

"My mother's Book of the Month Club sent it, and I like stories about war."

"What about the Rhett and Scarlett story? That's a big part of the novel. What did you think?"

"I thought it was good."

I thought it was great. I've always enjoyed love stories. I thought Becky Thatcher was the best thing about *Tom Sawyer*. I didn't mention that, because boys are supposed to prefer adventure stories. But I liked both the same.

"What about writing? Do you like to write?"

"It's okay." Three years ago, I bought an old Remington typewriter for five dollars and wrote war stories. Captain Nelson was always my main character. I would've mentioned that, but I didn't think he'd really be interested in my war stories.

"Why do you think you do so poorly in school, Jamie?"

"I don't do well on tests."

"Why is that?"

"I don't study."

"Why is that?" He smiled and then I smiled, because I realized I wasn't answering his question.

"I have trouble concentrating on things I don't like. I like to read our class short stories, but I don't like memorizing."

I hated memorizing catechism answers, but I wouldn't mention that to him, either. And I hated short-answer questions. I liked paragraph writing. Little by little, I was able to figure out the answer. It was easier than short-answer questions.

"He daydreams, Brother. He's not lazy. He's smart. But he daydreams. He's always daydreamed."

My mother, who was sitting next to me and hadn't said a word during my interview, spoke up and surprised Brother.

"I'm sorry. I know this is his interview, but he won't tell you that he's a dreamer. Ever since he was a little boy, he's daydreamed. He can look at you and nod to make you think he's listening, but he's not. He's a cowboy. Isn't that right, Jamie?"

That embarrassed me. I was thirteen.

"Is that true, Jamie?" Brother looked very interested.

"Yea . . . yes."

But I wasn't about to mention that I also enjoyed daydreaming about Darlene on the Mickey Mouse Club or Lia, my next door neighbor. My mother was right. It was all the same thing, and it started a long time ago. My Aunt Louisa was the first person to catch me. I didn't even know I was doing it when she told me I wasn't listening.

Brother began to smile. "You're not daydreaming now while we're having this conversation? Why is that?"

"I don't know, Brother."

But I did know. I didn't daydream when I was with my friends or when I was reading a book. And I wasn't daydreaming here, because I enjoyed the attention I was getting. I liked this man and I wanted to go to his school.

"If you come to St. Edmund's, will you apply yourself?"

"Yes, Brother." I meant it.

"No daydreaming."

"No, Brother." I'd really try.

"Whatever you do, now, don't stop daydreaming altogether. You just learn when to do it. Writing stories is a good time. Okay?"

"Yes, Brother." No one ever told me it was all right to daydream before. I just couldn't do it in class.

"Oh, one more thing. I understand you know French but won't speak it." Father Quinn really had filled him in.

"Yes, Brother."

"Well, I'm sorry to say that we don't offer French. It's a beautiful language. But we're too small a school. You'll study Latin and Spanish."

We didn't study any language in grammar school, so I didn't care about that. But I was happy that he had mentioned it. I knew he said that for my mother, and again he made her happy.

Since St. Edmund's had a pool in the basement and a swim team, I joined immediately. I was a good swimmer and wanted to be around the brothers after school. On the first day of tryouts, I became good friends with Tom McMullen. Tom also sat next to me in class and was my first friend from the Bronx. During our first week on the team, we became friendly with a tall senior, the team's manager.

Carrying a clipboard and taking notes, this friendly senior spent a lot of time with our coach, Brother McKenna, who always singled him out for a conversation, and we'd hear them laugh together. Brother McKenna didn't laugh much with the other kids on the team. This senior wasn't a swimmer; but he wore sweats, so we figured he had to be the team's manager. He never told us his name, and we didn't ask, because he was a senior paying attention to us.

In freshman year, all the seniors looked like grown men to me, and he even had the shadow of a beard. When he spoke to us, we listened. During our first swim meet with Brooklyn Prep High School, Tom and I laughed when their divers couldn't deal with the pool's low ceiling and hit it with their feet.

Sitting behind us, our friend the senior tapped us on the shoulders and shook his head, and we stopped laughing. That was my first lesson in school sportsmanship. This was high school, and I wanted to be mature and a good sport. I thought it was still funny, but I never laughed again.

When I swam the backstroke for my event, he was there at the end of the pool to congratulate me—and help me out of the water. Despite my being in good shape—since we did a hundred laps a day at practice after school—I was exhausted.

The chlorine and all the cheering made me dizzy. Enclosed pools magnify everything, because there are tiles on all the walls and floor.

At the end of the race, I hit the wall, turned, and grabbed it. Hanging on, I floated awhile until I heard, "Good going, Lachlan. You came in second."

I had no idea who was where in the race. I just wanted to finish. I could hardly move my arms. When I looked at the lights around the pool, they were surrounded by small rainbows, and then I saw a shadow lean over me.

"No nap floating, Lachlan." I grabbed the senior's hand.

That was my first meet, and my last, because of a skin allergy to the chlorine in the water. Since the seniors and freshmen were separated by three floors, I didn't see "our senior" for a while. Tom said he hadn't seen him at the pool, either. When we did see him again, I thought of Jackie Cooper, the famous child actor on television.

My mother bought our Motorola TV in 1956, and I'd stare at anything that appeared inside the "box." I was one of the last kids on the block to have one. Even my friend Walter had one, while his mother still used the icebox in the summer and the fire escape in the winter for her milk and vegetables. They had to share the hall bathroom with three other apartments on their floor, but they had their own television set in the kitchen, their warmest room in the winter.

When I wasn't playing punchball or touch football in the street, I did my homework on the floor in front of the TV. And since I was very young, I watched all the cartoon shows, Abbott and Costello movies, and "Our Gang" with Jackie, Farina, Chubby, and Wheezer.

In the "Teacher's Pet" episode, Jackie Cooper complains to a woman, who has given him a lift to school, about losing his beloved teacher, Miss McGillicuddy. She was leaving the classroom to get married. Not realizing that this sweet blonde woman is his new teacher, he has nothing nice to say about this "Miss Crabtree," who he says is an "old battle-axe."

When he sees the new teacher walk into the classroom and introduce herself, he's embarrassed and ashamed. She's the woman who just gave him a lift. She's Miss Crabtree. And she's beautiful. He leaves the room, sits under a tree, and cries until she brings him a piece of cake and ice cream; and he tells her that she's "prettier than Miss McGillicuddy."

I never had a teacher who gave us ice cream and cake on any day of school, and I never thought of nuns as pretty—or not pretty—but I enjoyed believing a Miss Crabtree could be teaching somewhere. I also liked the surprise ending. O. Henry stories were my favorite.

One morning in my Latin class, Tom and I became Jackie Cooper of "Our Gang." Wearing the collar and black robe of a brother, Brother Franco—our senior and friend, the student manager of the swim team—walked into the room.

He apologized to the class for missing the past two weeks, but he was sure that Brother Burns, our substitute teacher, had done a good job. Brother Burns was a good teacher, and at the time, I was sorry that he wasn't our permanent teacher, who was in charge of the school's bookroom and would return shortly.

When our permanent teacher turned out to be "Miss Crabtree," I turned to Tom and, with raised eyebrows, gave him a "what-do-you-think-of-that?" face. And, with squinted eyes, Tom made a "did-we-say-anything-we-shouldn't-have?" face. I shrugged, Tom shrugged back, and Brother Franco laughed.

He knew what we were thinking, and he knew what we were thinking last week at the pool, because he played along with us while he was helping Brother McKenna after school. But at the same time, he was teaching us. Well, that was it for me.

I was sure of three things: I was going to enjoy Latin; I was going to be a mature high school freshman; and I was going to become a brother.

Rosie and Diana

The week before my first high school dance at Most Precious Blood, a girls' high school on 78th Street, I wasn't so sure I wanted to be a brother. I was fourteen and had just discovered that brothers couldn't marry; they couldn't even date. I had never seen a brother before high school, so I didn't know this. I knew priests couldn't marry.

But why couldn't brothers? They couldn't change bread and wine into the body and blood of Christ. They couldn't hear Confession. We knew nuns took a vow of chastity, because they told us so. I figured they just didn't want to get married. Nuns didn't seem to like us boys much.

I wasn't so sure I liked the idea of taking a vow of chastity. Going to school in the morning, I looked at the girls on the Lexington Avenue bus and had trouble finishing my homework. Many of them were very pretty, and like the girls in my class last year, some even wore uniforms. But these girls were different, mysterious, and I wanted to know them.

Why were they smiling? Did they have boyfriends? Maybe they were thinking about me. I pretended to do my homework and be mysterious for them.

I had never thought much about the girls in grammar school. Not in that way anyway. I rarely looked at them. I'd known them my entire life, so I knew too much about them, and they knew too much about me. Some of them were taller than I was, and a few were faster runners. But these girls on the bus were strangers, and since I really looked at them, I noticed that many of them had really good figures. Some of these girls in Catholic school uniforms might be going to the Friday night parish dances in the neighborhood.

The dances were always formal. My first nighttime dress-up. Wearing my new school sport coat and tie—and *boss* gold socks—in the evening was a new experience. The dance took place in the school's auditorium, which reminded me a little bit of the schoolyard, because the girls stood in groups of girls, and the boys stood in groups of boys. But this was different, because we were there to be together.

We sneaked looks at one another. When I noticed a girl looking at me, she'd turn her head, and I did the same when I got caught. I didn't want her to think I liked her. And, of course, there was no schoolyard shouting. There was music. Not Rosemary Clooney or Frank Sinatra music. Our music.

Here tonight, we were not sitting around, listening to 45s on a record player at home or to WABC 770 on the stoop. Loud rock-and-roll guitars and drums surrounded us here, and I was nervous and excited at the same time. I was in the fifth grade play, *Show Boat*, again. Watching the curtain go up and seeing the stage lights, I felt the same way. Even in the back row.

Red, blue, green, and yellow spots swept across the floor and walls from a rotating speckled globe on the ceiling. The light was low, and since I never wore my glasses outside school, I couldn't see any faces. But I could see girls putting their hands in front of their faces to hide what they were saying. I thought that was funny. Who could hear them? I couldn't hear the boy next to me. And even if I could read lips and brought my glasses, who could see lips?

Once the older boys began to ask the girls to dance, I made my move. Since I had come alone, I looked for a girl who was alone, but there wasn't one. When I looked to the right near the stage, I saw two girls who weren't taller than I was. I was still short for my age. They looked friendly. They never covered their faces with their hands. When they fast-danced with each other, they reminded me of Sherri dancing with her friends on the street. Girls were good dancers.

Once I decided the song was a slow dance, I quickly walked to the two girls before it was over and stuck out my hand to the one who didn't look away when she saw me coming. She took my hand. She didn't smile, but I didn't smile first.

I led her to the middle of the dance floor and faced her. We were still not smiling. This was serious. She wasn't dancing to a fast song with a girlfriend, and I was dancing with a person

I didn't know. Really dancing. Another first. I was a teenager now, and everything was going to be different.

Although the song "Angel Baby" was half over when we started to dance, I could still hear the opening guitar chords, which had made me conscious of each step I took across the dance floor. Then I was holding her and listening to the singer say that her heart "skips a beat," because "you are near me." One, two . . . I would have fallen in love with any girl that night, but I was dancing with this girl. One, two . . . Now, I was someone's angel baby.

It wasn't coincidental; it was fate. I fell in love with this girl before I knew who sang "Angel Baby." When I asked for her name, she said, "Rose—without the Originals" and laughed. That surprised me, because I hadn't seen her smile yet. One, two . . .

"Originals?"

"That was Rosie who just sang 'Angel Baby.' We're dancing to her song. I'm just joking. We have the same name, that's all." Rose was sweet. One, two . . .

"Yeah . . . funny," I said.

No, I hadn't made the connection. I was thinking of my steps and looking at her pretty face. At the end of the song, she thanked me and walked back to her friend. There was nothing really funny about it. She was just being cute. Then I thought of Sherri, because Rose looked a little like Sherri. They both had long brown hair.

Last summer, I'd watch Sherri dance near the corner with the other girls, and she'd watch me watching her—but I never danced with her. I had never really danced with any girl before. I liked to tease Sherri and her friends. I was the best gorilla knuckle-walker on the block, and the girls screamed when I chased them. I'd roar and pick up one girl, then another, so that it wasn't obvious I wanted to pick up Sherri.

Both Rose and Sherri had dark eyes, and both were as tall as I was. Rose looked older, probably because she was a year ahead of Sherri, who was in the eighth grade this year. They both came here to Precious Blood. That bothered me a little, because it was a small school, and they probably knew each other.

But being here with Rose was serious. We had held each other. I didn't need to be King Kong. I didn't need to dance with every other girl there just to dance with her. I had picked her and she said yes. I was there to meet girls, and I met her right away. That was fate.

But I came prepared. I had watched "American Bandstand" after school, so I'd know how to move. It was all perfect. Rosie was right when she sang, "It's just like heaven, being with you, dear." I was in heaven and she was, too, I think, because I felt her body against mine—and I forgot all about Sherri while we were dancing.

I never danced with Rose again. I never had the chance, because she danced every other dance with another boy. Once they started, they never stopped. They danced and talked, and sometimes they didn't even separate after the song had ended. They held each other and only moved for the next dance. If the song was fast, they walked off the dance floor and held hands by the stage.

I was never her angel baby. He was and I hated him. He was taller than I was. And bigger. Maybe older. They probably had known each other before the dance; Rose had picked him before she had a chance to know me. That made me feel a little better, but I left anyway. It was still early, and maybe Sherri was around.

There was something fateful in meeting her and then watching them together, because the following Monday morning, I saw Rose's boyfriend by the soda machine in our cafeteria. He was a sophomore at St. Edmund's. In a strange way, Rosie and I were still connected. My mother would say it was meant to be.

Walking home that night, I decided to go to all the Friday night dances. High school girls were different from grammar school girls, and I wanted to go steady with one of them. My friend Ronnie was lucky. He had a girlfriend for a long time, and I think he liked Cookie more than he liked all of the guys put together. And one more thing: I enjoyed being with the brothers, but I would never become one. I knew that for sure now.

I continued to go to dances, and dancing with a girl I didn't know, a complete stranger, that September night changed everything. Girls were no longer grammar school classmates or the girls on the block. They were girls from Flatbush, Brooklyn and Woodside, Queens. They came from Castle Hill in the Bronx. They even came from the neighborhood, but I'd never seen them before. They were exotic.

Now I thought about girls all the time and lost interest in songs like "The Battle of New Orleans." I wanted to hear "Lonely Boy" and "Come Softly to Me." I was a teenager in love with girls—and with love—and would have to wait for the last dance of the year to meet another girl like Rose.

When I didn't go to Precious Blood, I went to the Friday night dances at St. Mark's, a girls' school on Lexington Avenue. I was no longer the loner; I traveled with the guys, and that made meeting girls in groups easier—and safer. All for one, one for all. Even though we didn't shave, we all wore Old Spice or Canoe. I wore Old Spice, because I thought it was manlier.

I was also wiser. I still couldn't do the fast-dances, but I recognized the slow ones before the middle of the song. If I couldn't figure it out, I'd ask one of the guys. Someone would know.

"Is this slow?"

"I'm not sure."

"Yeah, yeah. Let's go."

Daniel was right most of the times. Pretty soon, we all knew, because they'd play the same popular songs every Friday.

I still never wore glasses at a dance. Why would I wear them here? I'd never ask a girl with glasses to dance with me.

"She's good looking . . . right?" I'd ask a friend.

"She's okay."

After a while I knew who was trustworthy. Some guys thought it was funny to trick a friend. I played a joke on Archie once—and he got even with me. Because of him, I tried to slow-dance with a girl to "Will You Still Love Me Tomorrow" by the Shirelles. After an awkward thirty seconds of trying to follow me, she gave me a look and walked away. Archie got a good laugh that time.

It was fate again that I'd meet a girl at the last dance of the year. I met Rose at the first dance and hadn't felt the same way, until I was someone's angel baby again. It was June, and we had just finished our Regents Exams. I had done well. For the first time in nine years, I knew for sure I'd passed all my end-of-year tests. My friends and I were going to Far Rockaway Beach in the morning to celebrate.

I met her at St. Mark's, and we liked each other immediately. I never danced with a girl twice in a row. But we did. After the first dance, we exchanged names and schools. She was a student here at St. Mark's. Then another song started. It seemed natural to dance again. We both stood there, and something told me she wanted me to ask her again. I reached for her hand, and she nodded and smiled.

After the dance I thanked her and walked away. I didn't want her to think I was that interested. But I was. Her name was Diana. She had red hair, and even without glasses, I could see her on the other side of the hall. She was the only girl there with red hair. I thought of the beautiful actress who was a good tipper and lived up the block. I delivered medicine and perfume to her for the drug store. She and Diana had the same color hair.

To make Diana think I was popular, I danced with another girl I met a few dances back. Alice was a nice girl, but she wasn't exciting or different. She liked me, I could tell, but I never got butterflies or lightheaded dancing with her, and no priest or nun ever told us to move apart for the Holy Ghost.

"Now, keep your distance and let the Holy Ghost breathe."

In a way, she reminded me of the girls from grammar school. She was very sure of herself. Even her dress looked like a uniform. Last year, she was probably the smartest eighth grader in her school. I liked her, but I knew she was smarter than I was.

I asked Diana to dance again, and this time, a priest told us to make room for the Holy Ghost. Twice. But we had only three dances before they played "Shout!" and everyone shouted with the Isley Brothers. Jumping up and down, Diana and her friend ran onto the dance floor, and after "Shout!" they fast-danced a few more times. Daniel joked that the Holy Ghost was playing the records.

As soon as I heard a slow dance, I hurried across the dance floor, and she smiled and took my hand. I finally had a girlfriend. We danced a few more times, and before I left, I asked Diana for her phone number. Another big first.

"I'm leaving, Diana. What's your number?"

"Why? The dance isn't over yet."

"We're going to the beach tomorrow. Early."

"Well, it was nice meeting you."

"Can I call you?"

"Yeah, sure."

I came prepared with pen and paper. We said goodbye and she turned to dance with her friend. It had taken me the whole school year, but I went home with a girl's phone number. And it took me a very long time to fall asleep. Behind a chain-link fence, Diana was watching me hit home runs in a championship game. Rounding the bases, I watched her watching me. I really had a girlfriend.

As soon as we got back from the beach, I called her. My friends had told me to wait.

"Play hard to get."

"Yeah, good idea, Butchie."

But I couldn't. Suffering with my first sunburn of the year, I called her from the drugstore phone booth. There was no privacy in our apartment—unless my mother was cooking in the kitchen.

I placed a dime and five nickels for extra minutes on the shelf under the phone and pulled the accordion door shut. I was nervous and wasted my first dime on a wrong number. Then I dropped two nickels in the slot. Again the same wrong number, same person. I apologized, but he was annoyed. I had fifteen cents left.

This time, I said the telephone numbers aloud twice before I dialed. "A . . . A . . . S . . . S . . . 4 . . . 4 . . ."

"Check the phonebook, will ya!" Same guy.

I had written down the wrong number. I was nervous and it was dark. I wasn't wearing my glasses. She spoke quickly and the music was loud. It was getting late. I was love-dizzy. Now I'd have to wait for September to see her again—unless I could figure out the right combination.

The next morning, while my sunburnt friends and I sat in Charlie's hallway—still our favorite hangout on hot and cold days—we worked out the combinations of the last four numbers. She had told me that she lived in Astoria, Queens, so it had to be "AS-4." I was sure the following numbers were correct, but I must have switched two of them. Calling all those combinations would be expensive.

"I know how to get her number." We looked at Daniel.

"Archie's sister worked the window." Archie's older sister went to St. Mark's, and she was a class officer.

"What? She knows every redhead at St. Mark's?"

We all laughed, but she probably did. How many redheads could there be in a small school?

"No, she collected the ID cards, remember? It was the last dance of the year? How many Dianas from Astoria were at the dance?"

"Our phone numbers are on those cards!" I yelled. Daniel didn't answer. As usual, he was way ahead of me.

Of course, he was right. There was only one Diana who lived in Astoria. Diana Collins. She also went to St. Mark's, and she had red hair. And now I had her number. She had given me a fake one. The last two numbers were totally different. Daniel had saved me a pocketful of dimes.

I never called. Instead I took the subway to her apartment building the next morning. Her last name and address were listed on the card. I rang the "Collins" bell for the apartment under the stairs. Her father was the superintendent of the building. The door near the stairs opened immediately, and Diana walked out of her apartment. Wearing a white top and shorts, she was eating a thick slice of watermelon, almost the color of her hair. The light was at my back, so she walked up to me. When she recognized me, she stopped and spoke through the slice.

"How did you find me?" Under her surprised blue eyes, the watermelon looked like a mask.

"Why did you give me a fake number?"

"How did you find me?"

"Why did you give me a fake number?"

"How . . . I don't know."

Then it didn't matter, because I had found her, and she was happy I had. I could tell by the way her hand moved in mine. We walked around her neighborhood for a while, and then after making the sign of the cross, we sat on the steps of a nearby church. We couldn't stop talking about "that night" and her "crazy mistake."

"My father's very strict."

We listened to her radio, and I thought about Paul Anka's song "Diana." But I didn't mention it, and I hoped they wouldn't play it. Rosie's "Angel Baby" and Rose didn't work out for me last September. Superstition ran in my family.

Before I left that night, we kissed under the hallway stairs. That was her idea. She took my hand and led me there. I was nervous about someone—like her father—coming out her door; it was two feet away. She said no. He was fixing a sink in an apartment upstairs. She had checked with her little sister.

Then we did it. It was better than a "Truth-Dare-Consequences-Promise-or-Repeat" kiss, because we wanted to do it. It was the most exciting kiss of my life, because we wrapped our arms around each other. And, of course, it was the longest kiss of my life. Then I asked her to "go steady" with me.

She lowered her head and nodded yes.

We kissed again, and that was even sexier, because it was a "French Kiss," another first for me. I didn't like the name, but the kiss was so personal and exciting that I pulled her to me. I could even feel the top of her legs pressing against mine. But we stopped, because I moved away. I heard a door opening somewhere upstairs. I looked up and she shook her head no. She wanted to kiss again, but I couldn't stop thinking about her father. I didn't like fathers much. Next time, we'd go to the movies.

I thought about her all the way home. She was perfect. She was pretty and sweet. She was very daring. Even wild. She wore a white top and shorts—and ate watermelon—and kissed me in her own building while her father was working above us. And as far as I could tell, she was a perfect French kisser.

Six days later, she broke up with me on the telephone. Her father didn't like me, she said, because I wasn't from the neighborhood. That was the reason he gave her. I figured he was probably worrying about my impure thoughts. I had many, especially about Diana. But even if I were from the neighborhood, he wouldn't have liked me. I didn't like him much either, but he had the right idea about me and my thoughts.

By that time, I didn't care anyway. She didn't seem to care much, either. She didn't cry; she didn't even sound sad. The trip across the river to Queens each day made going steady difficult. And it was expensive. The subway was fifteen cents each way, and the movie tickets and soda added up. I needed a girlfriend closer to home. During the following year, I saw Diana at most of the dances. She still loved to fast-dance. We said hello but never danced again.

During the past year, I had discovered many things about myself. For the first time in my life, I could be a good student. I liked Latin, English, and history, and I even did well in math, because I had Brother Doyle, the best teacher in the school. But as much as I liked him and the other brothers, I could never become one. Even though I learned that going steady wasn't that steady, I liked French kissing and the idea of being someone's angel baby.

Looking at girls doing homework on buses or walking with their friends on the street made me happy. We were in high school now, and thinking about girls was easier than not thinking about them—and more fun than looking at naked natives in *National Geographic* magazine and posters of Brigitte Bardot. Girls were everywhere, and next year, I'd learn a new dance and twist with other girls like Rose and Diana.

Garden of Eden, 1961

In January of 1961, I was fifteen and a sophomore at St. Edmund's, and tomorrow morning, the principal was going to expel me. Our mid-term examinations would begin on Wednesday. Two a day—for three days. It was Monday night, and when I wasn't staring at my Latin spiral notebook, I was staring at the telephone next to me. It was going to ring. Brother Shaye, my principal, was going to call my mother. When I wasn't staring at the notebook or the phone, I watched my mother set the table in our small kitchen. Every day, she came home from work at six o'clock and prepared a meal for our family of two. I felt awful.

If you sat at one corner of our studio, you could see the entire apartment. And that's where I sat. Near the phone. If you wanted privacy, you shut the kitchen door—or sat in the bathroom. Those rare times I called a girl, I'd ask my mother to sit in the kitchen with the door closed. Not for long. Just long enough for me to stutter through a written script of questions.

"Do you have homework tonight?"

We always had homework. I hadn't mastered open-ended questions, yet.

"Would you like to see *West Side Story* Saturday night?"

I always had a backup movie. Movie marquees changed frequently back then, so there was a good chance I wouldn't need *Breakfast at Tiffany's*.

If my mother was busy in the living room, I'd go to the corner drugstore and use the phone booth. I'd sit on the small seat, close the accordion door, place my script and dime—and a few optimistic nickels—on the shelf under the phone for a longer conversation, take a deep breath, and blow through tight lips for several seconds.

With script in hand, I'd dial. Of course, I never got past the dime and one nickel. To this day, I have trouble speaking on the phone with strangers. If I called a girl for a date, she was a stranger. As a result, I knew very little about the opposite sex. I knew almost nothing.

Brother Shaye would find my admission about the opposite sex incredible. Pure fiction. But it wasn't fiction and—considering my transgression—his disbelief was well-founded. I was guilty as sin. Brother Delaney, my English teacher, would call me a paradox.

My mother had no idea that she was going to receive terrible news. Tonight would change my life. Our lives. When that phone rang, I would become a public school student, and we Catholic school kids knew they were "inferior." We had known that since grammar school. The nuns always made references to public schools.

"The poor unfortunates. They're receiving an ungodly education. You're very fortunate children."

More important, my mother would be very disappointed. She paid the school's tuition of fifteen dollars a month, because she wanted the best for me. Since my father never paid alimony, that was a luxury.

Earlier this morning, I had no idea that I might be having my last smoke and cup of coffee at the corner diner, our off-limits hangout. Every morning before school, my friends and I broke a school rule and met at the end of the soda counter for coffee, jelly doughnuts, and urgent teenage conversation.

"Did anyone see 'Gunsmoke' Saturday night?" Many of us had.

"Anyone see *The Hound of the Baskervilles*?" We hadn't, but we had recently read Doyle's novel in class and were looking forward to the movie.

"Sherlock is way too cool for crooks."

We *grubbed* cigarettes from one another and complained about homework and part-time jobs, girlfriends and not having girlfriends. Those sitting on the red-cushioned silver stools copied homework on the counter between cups of coffee and toast; and others leaned against the partition and drank their Cokes, because the diner was so crowded with students and neighborhood people.

At a quarter to nine, we picked up our books and left for school, one block away. There were no surprises, and life was simple. But this morning, I had no idea that I would never enjoy this ritual again.

Every morning, we walked past Brother Shaye standing between the only entrance to the school and his office. Sometimes he'd smile and say something, but usually he just watched over us, letting us know that he was always there—that he knew all of us personally. Today he sounded angry.

"Step lively, Morales. Let's go. You'll be late three days in a row."

This was *his* school, and we were *his* students. With arms akimbo, Brother had a mission. We were going to succeed in life.

"Lachlan." I turned. "In my office. Now."

Brother and I had a neighborhood connection. His brother had married the daughter of Mrs. Whelan, who lived down the street from me. On summer evenings for entertainment, people sat on stoops and beach chairs. My connection with Brother Shaye sat on her stoop, often with her husband and other daughter; and when I passed her, she always asked, "How's Mama?"

My knowing them made me different from the other boys. Nuns and brothers never spoke about their private lives to us, but I knew Brother Shaye's relatives. I was very proud of that. And after eight long years of nuns, I needed a male role model—so I adopted him. But we had never spoken about his family, my neighbors, and he had never called me into his office.

I stood in front of the counter and waited for the first bell, then the second bell. I watched his cheerful secretary, Mrs. B., type with one finger and whistle. When the halls were quiet, she stopped whistling, and I heard Brother.

"Hurry up there, Madden. You're late."

"Sorry, Brother. It was the bus."

"Take the train." His first period teacher would take care of this tardiness.

"Logan, fix your tie and tuck that shirt in. The other side. And you're also late. Twice this week. Detention. See me after school."

"Yes, Brother."

I turned to my left and watched him walk past me. He wasn't smiling. My mother thought he was too handsome to be a brother. She said that he had laughing eyes. Dark laughing eyes. Not today. They were just dark.

"I know what you did last week. Give it to me."

I became very small and cold. I knew what he wanted, and without saying a word, I gave him Lola's number. I felt a fear that I hadn't felt since living with my father.

"You are a disgrace to yourself—and this school. You are not to attend class. You are not to eat lunch with the other boys. I do not want you near them. You will sit on the bench outside this office and speak with no one. You will go home at 3:00, and I will call your mother tonight. Now go to the bench."

I think the whole school knew. I had shown the number to some friends, who told their friends, and some of them were still talking about me on the subway. I was only fifteen, and I had a prostitute's phone number. I had become a hero to most of the boys. In school, they whispered my name.

Last Friday on the subway going home, they hadn't whispered, and they hadn't noticed Father Brooks, the priest who heard our weekly confessions every Friday morning in school. Since there was no Seal of the Confessional, he was not bound to confidentiality; and he called Brother Shaye, because I was a dangerous influence on the other boys in his school.

Too bad I had missed confession last week.

I was allowed to buy a sandwich in the cafeteria, but I had to eat it on the bench. I was not to speak to any other student. When the lunch bell rang, the boys left the cafeteria in double file—in silence, as usual—and walked up to the fourth floor and higher for their afternoon classes.

My friends looked at me. They squinted and cocked their heads for answers. Some smiled hello. But some remembered that their unsmiling classmate on the bench had been a hero last Friday. Without smiles, they gave me low waves of a hand. Sympathy waves. I would never see them again.

But again on Tuesday, I sat on the bench. I was missing both days of review and would probably miss the examinations. But I still studied, because I needed something to do. Brother hadn't called last night. He would tonight. At three o'clock, Mrs. B. sent me home. I wondered if she knew. I hoped not.

I spent another night watching the phone, my mother, and my notebook. But the phone never rang. That wasn't unusual in those days. The television set was still a miracle and dominated our lives. Good thing, too. Imagine if the phone—next to me—had rung several times during the evening. I was spared those cold chest waves. I called Daniel, and he knew not to call. When I went to bed, my mother still didn't know. When I said goodnight, I wanted to tell her.

"Mom, Brother Shaye is calling, and he's going to kick me out of school, because I had a prostitute's phone number."

How could I tell her that? That would be too embarrassing and not the entire truth. I had called her. I had called a prostitute. Last Thursday night, we had met Archie's brother on Third Avenue. Joey was two years older than we were and thought he knew everything. When he quit school in the middle of his junior year, he got a good job in construction. Soon he'd be in the electrician union and set for life. A guy at work had given him the number, but Joey never called. He had a girlfriend.

"You guys should call. You could use a little love. When was the last time you had 'real' girlfriends?"

He was talking to Daniel and me, because Archie had already had two real girlfriends. My last girlfriend was Diana from Astoria, and she was "almost real" for only two weeks; and Daniel said he had a hand-holding girlfriend at summer camp last year. Joey was right about us. We were "sweet virgins."

But that wasn't the reason we called . . . I called. Since I lost the coin flip, I had to telephone her. One tail . . . two heads. I was tail. And I called, because we had to find out if it was true. After all, this was a prostitute, not a "who'er," not a girl who let you go almost all the way with her behind stairs in some hallway. I didn't know any girls like that. Diana knew how to make out, but that was it.

We went to the drugstore, where we made all our important phone calls. I sat in the phone booth and kept the door open, so Daniel and Archie could lean in to listen. I made believe I wasn't nervous as I was dialing, but hearing a voice after only one ring, I pulled the phone away from my face.

"Hello? . . . Hello?"

"Yes, is th-th-this L-Lola? . . . Hello, Lola?"

My heart was pounding, and I was speaking too fast. I had to slow down to control my stutter. Calling any girl I didn't know would have been difficult enough, but this was a woman, a prostitute.

"Yes, it is. Who is this please?"

She had a nice voice, very polite. Not like Sunny in *The Catcher in the Rye*, which I had read last summer. I read it in a day, and it became one of my favorite books.

"This is Ralph, and I was told to call this number if I wanted a good time." Joey had coached us.

"That depends, Ralph. Who gave you the number?" She knew my name wasn't Ralph.

"Tommy D. from Houston Street." That was the password. I didn't know if there really was any Tommy D.

"Well, what can I do for you, honey?" That was good enough for her.

"How much is it?" I shut my eyes, because I was going too fast. There should have been another question first.

"For what, honey? Round-the-world or a quickie?

"Round world?"

"No, honey. Round . . ."

I started to laugh and hung up.

"Why'd you hang up?" That was Daniel.

"What's a round world?"

"It's round-the-world, you virgin dope. It means doing everything." That was Archie.

111

I couldn't call her back, but that night I couldn't fall asleep for a long time. I thought about round-the-world and Lola, who lived on the West Side, one short bus ride through Central Park.

I skipped going to the diner the next morning and went straight to school, straight to the bench. Brother had said speak to no one, and that's what I did. My friends understood. They were going to make it easy for me. And they didn't want Brother's anger directed at them.

Either way, it did make it easier. I was not a hero anymore. We'd make eye contact, but there were no smiles. No waves. By this time, my offense was legendary. They were looking at a condemned man. All the boys knew, and some of the upperclassmen grinned. I was meeting my Maker right in front of them.

Wednesday morning, I returned to the bench. Again, Brother hadn't called. When the first bell rang at 8:55, he left his position by the entrance and walked to the office and—without looking at me—said, "Go to class."

I looked around to see if I was the one to go to class. I was. I was the only boy in the lobby. I turned to thank him, but he wasn't there. He was now speaking to Mrs. B. in the office. I stuck my head in the office.

"Thank you, Brother." He didn't turn around.

I ran up the five flights of stairs to the classroom. As I passed Brother's huge oak desk, he gave me the examination and two blue books for my essays. I hung my coat on the wall hook in the back of the room and sat at my corner desk. I looked down at the test paper and up at the bowed heads in front of me, and I realized Brother Shaye was not going to expel me. He wasn't even going to call my mother.

The test was difficult, because waves of relief distracted me. From the corner music store's loudspeaker, the Coasters sang "Splish Splash." We raised our heads and looked at the windows. I couldn't stop smiling. Brother had forgiven me.

"I was takin' a bath."

That made me almost as happy as my mother's not receiving his phone call of the terrible news.

At lunchtime, I returned to the bench with a sandwich, but Mrs. B. stuck her head out the door and said, "You can go back to the cafeteria, Mr. Lachlan. You don't have to sit here anymore."

Then she smiled at me. There was no way she knew about last week. Brother would never tell her. Never. As I walked to the cafeteria, I heard her whistling and typing.

But Brother hadn't forgiven me. When I entered the building the next morning, he was there; but he looked to my left, to my right, and over my head.

"Hurry, boys. You'll be late in two minutes."

I hurried with the others, but I knew I wasn't one of the "boys." He would never forgive me, and I understood. I deserved it. He hadn't told my mother, because he knew our situation at home. Like the sisters at St. Jude's, the brothers were tough but protective.

My mother and Brother Shaye met the summer before my freshman year. She thought he was very kind, and he thought she worried about me too much. That had to be the reason. He was not going to tell her that her son had acted on impure thoughts, dirty thoughts. He was protecting my mother.

For several cold winter months, I was invisible. Brother wasn't. I saw him in the morning, at lunch, and at the end of the day. He never said a word to me; he never looked at me. His last words to me back in January were, "Go to class." They had made me very happy then, but now I remembered only the words, "Go to the bench."

All the other brothers were fine with me. Maybe they didn't know. Maybe for my mother, he didn't tell them. But I was still a "disgrace," and after a while, I didn't care. I didn't need a role model anymore. I was doing well in all my classes. That was a big change from elementary school where I had daydreamed successfully for eight years and was often promoted "on trial" to the next grade.

Here in high school, I was a much happier student, who was transferred into the honors section on the first day of sophomore year. Before long, I had two sets of friends. The guys in the diner and the guys in class.

The diner guys were not in my honors class. They lived in Yorkville, a few blocks north of my neighborhood and were "street friends." We'd often meet up before parish dances on Friday nights and for courage drink a half-pint of Kentucky Gentlemen or Southern Comfort on some dark street near the church.

Between the stop-and-go traffic of Fords and Chevys, we played sewer-to-sewer touch football and punchball; but for some of us, doing "the Slop" and "the Watusi" was threatening. All the fast ones were, so we watched the girls dance with one another—and waited for "In the Still of the Night," or some other slow song, to make our moves. The nuns and priests made sure the dances weren't too slow.

"How do you expect the Holy Ghost to enjoy himself? Give him some room to move."

During the week after school, we often took the bus home together and, "cuffing" lit cigarettes in our pockets, showed our bus passes to the driver with the other hand. We walked to the back and sat near the open windows.

If the driver saw the smoke and yelled, "Put those out, or I'll come back there!" we'd throw them out the windows, and that would be it.

We broke the rules, and the driver was doing his job. He probably did the same thing when he was a kid. My Yorkville friends were tough but good kids. Some went to college, and some joined the army and went to Viet Nam a few years later. A few never returned.

My new "honors" classmates—my class friends—were going to college. They were more sophisticated than I was and knew that Dostoevsky was very different from our school authors and far more exciting because of the psychological realism of his novels.

But I quickly caught on. With the gas burners keeping me warm in the winter, I read *Crime and Punishment* in the kitchen, so I wouldn't disturb my sleeping mother. There were three of us who passed Dostoevsky's novels around, and I gave up my television shows to read *The Brothers Karamazov* and *The Idiot,* too. This was such a new experience that my not needing to consult the glossary for the Russian nicknames made me proud.

At school, I lived in two worlds and had the respect of both. I was grateful that Brother had spared me—and my mother—but we were no longer connected. And he became invisible to me.

I did very well in the spring. Brother Mahoney, my history teacher, made world events come alive with anecdotes and humor. He had no reservations about letting us know that he liked us.

"You guys are ugly, but the state examiner will overlook that if you keep your heads down and keep writing. Don't show your faces, and you'll do well."

My not being a "math student" didn't interfere with my geometry grades; I did well with Brother Doyle, too. After my exposure to Dostoevsky, though, my English reading assignments were easy but sometimes less satisfying. I was beginning to appreciate the value of knowledge for the first time in my life.

Coming into the building one Friday morning in May, I heard something I hadn't heard since that gray day in January. Brother Shaye's voice and my name.

"Lachlan, please go to my office."

He was looking at me, but he wasn't smiling. He didn't look angry, but he looked very serious. I walked into his office, and for the first time since that awful winter morning, I stood before the counter watching the secretary's finger hover over the keyboard.

"That was the second bell, DeSantis. You were absent yesterday."

"I was sick, Brother. Here's my note."

"All right. Not now. Show me after school."

"Okay, Brother."

While Brother Shaye was walking into the office, he began to speak, and Mrs. B. stopped whistling. He was speaking quickly, and by the time he rounded the counter, I knew he wanted me to do a "favor" for him.

"I'd like you to buy flowers. For Mrs. Kearney. She's the mother of one of the brothers at O'Connell High School."

O'Connell was another Catholic school, our traditional rival at the St. Patrick's Day Parade. I remember thinking then that all the brothers were probably really friends, and the rivalry was just a game among them. I was surprised and pleased. This was better than the brothers in our building pretending to feud with one another.

"Okay, fellows. Brother Franco thinks his Latin translation exercises are interesting, even exhilarating, so make the poor man happy and pretend they are. Do them right away and save *David Copperfield* for last . . . for the real fun tonight."

Of course, we'd laugh and wait for Brother Franco's response, and laugh again. But Brother Shaye was not smiling.

"Mrs. Kearney is a patient at Memorial Hospital," Brother continued. "She's very sick. If I give you five dollars, will you be able to go there this afternoon? She's very, very sick, I'm afraid."

"I'll go as soon as I get off the bus, Brother. What kind of flowers should I buy?"

"Cheerful ones. She's in room 330. And here's a note to give her with the flowers." He gave me an envelope with a five dollar bill. "Thank you, Lachlan." He turned and sat at his desk.

I put the envelope and money in my jacket pocket, and that afternoon, left the school with a mission. I could think of only one thing: I wasn't invisible. Brother had remembered that I lived near the hospital. On the bus I sat by an open window and saw people—block after block—sitting on stoops and standing in groups, enjoying the sunny spring afternoon. And I wasn't invisible.

I got off the Lexington Avenue bus two stops after mine and walked down 68th Street to buy the flowers in a little store on First Avenue. When the owner offered to help me, I told him I needed "cheerful flowers for a very sick lady at Memorial. Five dollars' worth." He nodded and said he had just the ones she'd like.

"We'll mix them up nice for her."

This was my first time in a florist. I didn't like the odor of flowers. They reminded me of my grammar school class going to a younger classmate's funeral to pray for her "eternal soul." At the time, I knelt at the coffin and stared at Harriet Birch, whose father I still see in his bakery around the corner. Today, when I pass a florist—or smell flowers in someone's house—I think of her surrounded by them.

I took the flowers and gave him Brother's money. I told him they were pretty, because he had helped me.

It would take me a couple of minutes to walk to Memorial. I liked hospitals. I was used to them. My mother worked at New York Hospital on York Avenue, and I'd visit her on days off from school. But this was my first time in Memorial.

It was smaller and less busy than New York Hospital, and when I stepped off the elevator on the third floor, I became aware of the silence. There were doctors and nurses moving about, but it was very quiet. Very serious. Most of the doors were closed, and I saw no patients. I whispered to the nurse at the desk for room 330, "Mrs. Kearney," and she directed me in a normal voice to the end of the hall.

On the bus coming down Lexington, I had wondered what Mrs. Kearney would be like. Probably very religious looking.

"Very sick," Brother had said.

We knew so little about the brothers at school that meeting a brother's mother seemed almost too personal. One Saturday morning last June, Brother Doyle had shocked us when he held a math review class in a T-shirt. And when he sat on his desk, we saw his ankles—another first. I had never seen a brother without his collar and robe.

Of course, in eight years of watching nuns, we children never saw more than hands and a square face that included chin, mouth, nose, eyes, and forehead. The eyebrows were my favorite. I stared at them, because I had always wondered if the sisters were bald.

Mrs. Kearney's door was open, and I stood there for a little while. She didn't look very sick, and for a brother's mother, she didn't look very religious. She looked like all the other old women in the neighborhood. But she looked very alone. There were two beds in her room, and the other one was empty. Hers was near the window, and there were flowers on the windowsill. I guess brothers from other schools had had the same idea. When I walked into the room, she was still staring out the window.

"Mrs. Kearney?" She turned her head.

"Yes, dear. I'm Mrs. Kearney."

She had deep blue eyes and a warm smile. In elevators, she probably made other people smile back. She lay on the window side of the bed, which looked too big for her. She lifted her arm and fluttered the back of her fingers at me.

"Come in. Please, come in." I liked her. "Come in, dear."

"I go to St. Edmund's, and my principal . . . Brother Shaye . . . asked me to give you these flowers . . . and this note."

"What's your name, dear?"

"Jamie. Jamie Lachlan."

I handed her the flowers and smiled. She carefully opened the envelope and read the note.

"How lovely, Jamie. Please thank Brother Shaye for me. He's such a nice man. Sit down, dear. Visit awhile. Will you? Do you have the time? Oh, good, just drag that chair over." She pointed to the chair near the window.

"That's right. Now isn't this lovely?"

For more than an hour, we could have been sitting in her kitchen. We spoke about school, and my mother, and the playground across the street on First Avenue. She wasn't from the neighborhood, but she could have been. She'd come here to Memorial so often, she said, that she knew it very well.

Sometimes she'd sit in the park and watch the children play in the sandbox. Sometimes she'd visit St. Jude's across the street and say a prayer at the Shrine of St. Jude Thaddeus. I knew the shrine at the back of the church well. When the sisters scolded us for bad behavior or poor grades, they recommended our lighting candles and praying to St. Jude. But it never seemed to help—even if he was the patron saint of lost causes.

"You better pray to our Blessed Mother as well, Jamie."

Mrs. Kearney knew the shrine well.

"It's such a beautiful church, isn't it?"

"It's my parish. That was my grammar school."

"Did you enjoy your time there, Jamie?"

"It's a good school. I met my best friend there . . . Daniel." That made her smile again, and making her smile made me happy. "And Mother Superior is a great principal."

"Oh, I'm very glad."

I never asked her how she felt, because I didn't want to remind her that she was sick—and she didn't look very sick. Just tired. And when she wasn't speaking, she was smiling. She seemed very interested in me.

"Tell me something, Jamie. Why did Brother Shaye choose you to bring me the flowers?"

"He knew I lived three blocks away."

"Are you the only boy at St. Edmund's who lives in the neighborhood?"

"No, Kevin and John live across the street. I went to grammar school with them, too."

"And he chose you of the three. He must think highly of you. I bet you're a very good student."

"I'm okay."

Oh, that was it. I was a better student than Kevin and John, but Brother probably knew they had afternoon jobs—and I didn't have one. He wanted Mrs. Kearney to get the flowers today. I was free.

"Well, it's a Friday afternoon—and look at that beautiful blue sky. I'm sure you'd rather be playing baseball with your friends, and I am a little tired, dear. Sounds funny coming from someone lying in a bed all day."

Then she looked at me and smiled.

119

"Thank you for coming, Jamie. Please don't forget to thank Brother Shaye for the flowers and for sending such a sweet boy with them. He's a kind man. You take very good care of yourself, dear."

I really had nowhere to go—and she was so easy to talk to—that I didn't mind sitting with her. I liked being around her. She sat up in the bed and reached out for both my hands and held them in hers for some time before we said goodbye. I walked back down the quiet corridor to the elevator. She did look tired. Maybe I'd go back and surprise her some other day. That made me feel better. I'd go back.

The following Monday, after my last morning cigarette with the guys at the diner, I walked into school and saw Brother with another student in his office. I'd have to wait for lunch, or the end of the day, to give him Mrs. Kearney's message. I wondered if he would thank me for taking the flowers to her. Maybe I'd be invisible again.

By the time I reached the stairs, I heard my name. I turned to walk back, but Brother was walking quickly toward me. He put his hand on my shoulder and gently turned me back to the stairs.

"No, keep going, or we'll both be late. I'll walk up with you. I need to see Brother Jaworski."

He didn't say another word until we reached the second floor. I had trouble keeping up with him.

"Thank you for being so kind to Mrs. Kearney."

"It was no big deal, Brother. I live only three blocks away."

"Anyone could have brought her the flowers. I chose you for a reason, and I was right to do so. She called me. She told me that you sat with her for some time. You made her very happy, Jamie. Very happy."

"She was a nice lady, Brother."

"Yes, she is, and that was very good of you, Jamie. Very kind." Suddenly, taking two steps at a time, he left my side.

"Brother is waiting for me—and don't be late yourself now, Lachlan."

Watching his back, I followed him up the steps. When he made the turn at the top and was out of view, I stopped. I fell back against the banister and listened to his footsteps above me. I was happy, but I couldn't smile. I was too surprised, too happy.

"I was never invisible."

We'll Always Have Today, 1970

"I see a telephone and it rings, but . . . no one speaks. And it rings . . . and rings. When someone picks it up to say hello, there is silence on the other end. Then, it rings again. But the caller does not speak."

Gina, Theresa's attractive fair-haired cousin with bright hazel eyes, was sitting on the floor, and the colorful cards were spread out in front of her. Theresa, my former student in New York, and her other cousins Benedict and Vincenzo were sitting on the couch. I sat on the antique rocker. When Gina mentioned the ringing phone and the silence, I stopped rocking. Gina was reading my cards. She bit the side of her lower lip and looked at me.

"Does this mean anything to you, Jamie?"

This card-reading session was meant to be entertainment. I expected to hear that I'd be wealthy and married to "la bellissima" Rachel, my traveling companion and girlfriend of two years. I'd have five beautiful children, who would look like Rachel, of course, and I would live for many happy years.

I never expected this.

"I think . . . you're seeing something that happened awhile ago. How could you know about that phone call . . . those phone calls, Gina? My friend Daniel knows about them, but I never told anyone else. How could you know about them?"

I never told Rachel and never would.

"I don't know, Jamie. The cards know. Who calls? Who doesn't speak?" Gina asked in Spanish.

She was Italian, and for the past week, her Roman family and she had shown Rachel and me a Rome not available to tourists. We ate fresh juicy figs bought from vendors on the street; and to stop the traffic on busy boulevards, the six of us held hands to make a laughing human chain. Since I didn't speak Italian, and Gina didn't speak English, we communicated in Spanish and French. I would then translate for Rachel, who was never far away.

"The person who calls is the person who doesn't speak. Which one are you, Jamie? You're the caller, aren't you? Why don't you speak? And now you are silent again. Why are you silent?"

The mystery and my reaction to it were upsetting Gina. In our week together, she had enjoyed the role of tour guide and teacher of her cousin's Spanish teacher in America. This charming young woman couldn't see the answer in the cards, but she wanted an answer for my silence now.

I shook my head. I didn't know what to say. Sitting back in the rocker on our last night in Europe, I became thoughtful and tense. I was no longer in Gina's living room. I was a college kid still living at home with my mother. I also wanted answers. What was going on here?

"Tell us, Jamie?"

I shrugged. Too personal. Too sad.

"What happened, Jamie? Please. I've never seen you like this." Now Rachel wanted to know.

Since we were flying back to New York early the next morning, Rachel and I said our goodbyes to a disappointed Gina and her wonderful family, and returned to our *pensione*, which Gina and Theresa had found for us near St. Peter's and the Vatican, close to Gina's apartment. There was packing to do, and I needed time to understand what had just happened.

After making the arrangements for the morning taxi to the airport and paying the charming concierge for our lovely modern room behind the ancient city wall facing the street, Rachel and I took a last look at the garden and its fountain of Venus and Adonis. Between two beautiful pines, we sat on the bench for our last impression of a Roman night when Rachel asked me about the phone call.

"Why didn't you speak, Jamie? What's going on? This is important to you, so it's important to me, and I'd like to know."

"That's just it, Rachel. I did. I did answer. I wasn't the caller. Look, this happened three years ago. It's not important anymore, and we need to get some sleep. I'm exhausted. Aren't you? How much wine did we drink tonight?"

"Eight bottles divided by . . ."

Rachel was a math teacher. Two years ago in 1968, we met at the orientation for New York City teachers. I was a high school Spanish teacher, who fell in love with the Spanish language and culture, because my high school principal gave me two chances to redeem myself. Thanks to Brother Shaye's kindness and patience, I became a good student. To be like him, I became a teacher. When I received my degree, he wanted to hire me; but at the time, there were no openings for Spanish teachers at St. Edmund's.

Rachel and I had had the first-day jitters. We weren't much older than our students. We were twenty-two, and after three dates in two weeks, we fell in love. No one was more surprised than I was. But yes, I loved Rachel, and she loved me. Even our students knew that.

"How come you're always with that cute math teacher, Mr. Lachlan?" They were having a good time with me. Her students gave her the same treatment.

"Hey, Miss B., what's going on with Mr. L. and you? I don't think you're telling us everything."

Back home in Manhattan, we still lived with our parents, but traveling together through France, Spain, and Italy, we had become family. Seven weeks in airports, train stations, hotel rooms, and restaurants will do that to fellow travelers; and eventually we accepted each other's odd behavior that had aroused intense interest during the first few days of the trip. We found new things to love about each other.

"Let's pack and go to bed. We'll get at least four hours of sleep."

After stuffing our four suitcases, one of them mine, we kissed goodnight and turned off the lights for the last time in Europe. Tomorrow, we would no longer be family—for now, anyway. This trip proved something to us about our being able to live together.

I thought I was sleepy, but hearing Rachel's light breathing and the noisy reconnaissance of a mosquito, I realized I was not going to sleep. Waving my hand in front of my face, I thought of her.

It was 1965, I was nineteen, an old teenager, and I was in love with Madeline Ferrara—Maddy—and she was in love with me. I remembered that long walk home. I remembered my happiness and the wonder of it.

"I have a girlfriend."

That's what I said aloud at three in the morning on First Avenue. I had just left Maddy outside her apartment door. We had been sitting on the steps between her floor and the one below so that her parents above and neighbors below couldn't hear—or see us. Suburban kids used cars for privacy; we used hallways.

Maddy and I talked, and kissed, and shared a cigarette, and kissed, and talked some more. When we said goodnight—this time, really for the last time—she stood two steps above mine, and I felt her warm cheek against my cheek, and we held each other. I wouldn't see Maddy until tomorrow.

Yes, I had a girlfriend. Her light-brown eyes were golden warm and inviting, and her hair was so dark that some said she dyed it. But no, her hair was natural. It was black and short. Very short. Maddy was Irish and Italian.

"A good mix," she said.

"A beautiful mix," I said.

Her laughter was irresistible. When she smiled or laughed, she turned her head to look into my eyes. She wanted to share everything with me. Even at the movies. We were one and that made me happy, and we smiled and laughed together. After nineteen years someone other than my mother loved me.

Before I met Maddy, my high school ring had become a symbol of my bachelorhood. It was my scarlet letter. I had read Hawthorne's novel in school and saw symbols everywhere. I put the ring in a desk drawer. Why should the world know what I knew? Telling Maddy that I needed her help to wash my apartment windows—while my mother was at work—I hoped to change its symbolism.

Other than our hallway hideaway and dark movie balconies, this meeting would be our first time alone. I wanted what most teenagers wanted in 1965.

"I got you to wear my ring," Sonny and Cher sang. "I got you, Babe."

Maddy and I met on a blind date and had been dating for four and a half months. That was a first. Most of my relationships rarely lasted beyond two movies, a hamburger at a nice diner, and a kiss gone wrong. The braces I wore during the first year of high school didn't help my confidence.

Some of my friends had girlfriends for years. Sitting on a stoop or an ash can, Ronnie enjoyed playing the henpecked boyfriend. He'd look at the invisible watch on his wrist.

"Fun's over, guys. The wife will be here in five minutes."

Sometimes she was "the ball-and-chain," "my old lady," or "the little woman." When Cookie turned the corner, he'd stand and stretch his arms wide, run his hand through his long hair, flick his cigarette over a parked car far into the gutter, walk up the street to meet her, and turn to us.

"See ya when I see ya, lonely boys."

After seeing a Saturday night movie at the RKO on 86th Street, couples went to McMurray's Bar & Grill and sat at a booth alone or with other couples. Girlfriends never came alone to the bar—or sat at the bar—and we single guys rarely sat in the booths. Eighteen got us draft cards, so we could drink legally, and no one ever proofed the girls.

Dropping quarters in the jukebox, playing table shuffleboard, or watching the Beatles on Ed Sullivan, we sat on the stools, paid fifteen cents for a small glass of beer, and ate strings of beef jerky.

But things would change when the discotheque scene moved uptown. The saloons and gin mills couldn't compete with the free music—and the women who wanted to meet men and dance. For them, we'd be willing to pay the fifty cents for a mug of beer. Hanging out at a "Singles Bar," we'd have to "get lucky." There were always women there.

This was going to be the big day. Everything was ready. Soda, potato chips, Windex. When the downstairs bell rang, I turned on the radio for atmosphere. I opened the door, and Maddy, arms crossed, was already there. She was smiling and looked beautiful. We kissed hello. In shorts and halter top, she was "ready to go to work."

"Let me at them."

I was ready for something else, but I dragged a kitchen chair to the window and climbed out onto the fire escape. She stood on her chair, sprayed the window, looked up, and asked if I had a ladder. Maddy was petite.

"A ladder? No, I don't have a ladder."

"How will I be able to reach up there?"

"Reach as high as you can, Maddy. I'll close my eyes. I've been washing windows since I was a kid." When she began to lift her arm above her head, she understood.

"I thought this window business was suspicious. Well, you're tall. When the time comes, I'll just sit on your big shoulders."

To "Help Me Rhonda," I sprayed and rubbed. Maddy sprayed, rubbed, and sang along with the Beach Boys.

When she heard Jagger sing, "Get Off My Cloud," she blew on the glass and swung her hands back and forth behind her shoulders and over her head. Standing on the chair, she was doing the "Jerk."

"You're missing the glass, Maddy."

"Dance with me."

I was a terrible dancer but somehow survived doing the "Jerk" and the "Twist," and she knew it.

"I'm in the public eye out here. People know me in this courtyard."

"You don't care what people think, do you?" She pouted.

"I do if they live next door, and I'm standing on the fire escape." I pouted back.

"Do you care what I think, Jamie?" Doing her Mick impersonation, she puffed her lips out and sang, "nooo satisfac . . ."

"Will you go steady with me?"

She stopped singing, and I could hear Mick still singing "Get Off My Cloud" on the radio. She made a what-did-you-say? face. Then she placed both hands on the glass. She looked serious. Too serious.

I positioned my hands over hers. I thought of those prison-movie visits and laughed. Now I was nervous. I should have waited, but it just came out. She was adorable.

"Maddy, will you go . . . ?"

"Yes, yes."

I climbed back through the window and stood on the chair with her, and we kissed in front of all the neighbors.

"Wait a minute. The ring—or the deal's off."

I hopped off the chair, took the ring out of the drawer, and gave it to her. I stopped smiling when she gave it back.

"Put it on my finger, please . . . hey, I could wear this on my ankle. That's okay. I got tape at home."

Maddy was sweet and funny, and she just loved me back.

That was this afternoon. Walking home on a dark and deserted First Avenue, I was now a "married man," and I was smiling. There were few cars going uptown, and most of the bars were closed or empty. The city was asleep, so I avoided stepping on the iron storefront basement doors.

At 79th Street, I looked up at the large clock over the bank's huge gold double doors. It was three, and we already had had our twelfth-hour anniversary. I never anticipated the next rush. Like my fire escape proposal, I never saw it coming. But this time, it was a whisper full of gratitude.

"Isn't this wonderful?"

The summer of '65 was the best summer of my life. I had a girlfriend and a job at the Grand Liquor Shop, a new store of fine wine on the East Side. The neighborhood was changing with the demolition of tenements and the construction of high rise buildings, the "white wedding cake" buildings up and down First and Second Avenues.

We were no longer the neighborhoods of Lenox Hill and Yorkville, where people sat at their windows or on stoops and beach chairs in front of buildings. And people drank more wine and less whiskey and beer. We were becoming the exclusive "Upper East Side" of Manhattan.

My $1.10 an hour minimum wage paid for our movie and dinner dates; the tips paid for birthday and Christmas presents. Ten cents was the usual tip, and a quarter was very good. Poor people, old people, and New York Hospital nurses down the street were the best tippers. If I had to choose between a six-story walkup and an elevator building, I'd pick the walkup anytime.

"After that long walk up here on this hot, hot day, would you like a nice cold glass of water?" There would also be a ten cent tip. Always.

Wealthy people were usually terrible tippers. At eleven p.m. on a cold Christmas Eve, I once bicycled ten blocks to Park Avenue with two cases of wine in the basket. The left hand held the top case in place; the right hand, the handlebar. After I locked the chain on the bike, I walked to the entrance, but the doorman intercepted me. He jerked his thumb to the service entrance on the left.

"Hey, kid, you know better than that."

When the customer answered the door, I followed him and carried the two cases past the laughing partiers in the living room to his enormous kitchen, where he thanked me, wished me a "Happy New Year," and gave me a quarter.

"See you next year!" He thought that was very funny. I smiled.

Bicycling in the light cold rain back to the store, I thought about seeing Maddy in an hour and exchanging gifts in her hallway. Lucky for us, all liquor stores had to be closed Christmas Day.

Then there were the homosexual men with the exclusive gift shop on Madison Avenue. We didn't use the word *gay*, because we didn't know it existed back then. We knew and used all the others, though. It was a mile bike ride, but a dollar tip was a sure thing, almost an hour's salary; and I could do it back and forth in twenty minutes. Smiling, I'd pedal in a snowstorm for them.

But my favorite customer lived in a large white doorman building with a bright red canopy. She was a prostitute. In the delivery boy's world, there are many stories about lonely beautiful women seducing lucky young men with packages.

"Yeah, she opened the door and had nothing on. I swear to God she had nothing on, and she wanted me. I swear to my mother."

I was never wanted by anyone. I had a seductive customer, but I never saw her. She lived across the street, but she never came into the shop. I delivered bottles of Scotch and bourbon to her several times a week. But she never answered the door. After two weeks, the doorman and I knew each other's names. I walked into the lobby, and Henry would call her apartment.

"Grand Liquor's here, Miss. Okay. Go ahead, Jamie."

"Thanks, Henry."

When I'd ring the 9A bell, a man, a different one each time, would open the door just enough to show half his face. The same arm paid me and took the bottle, and the door would begin to close.

"Did you give the kid a buck, Johnny?"

The door would reopen, and the arm, without the half face, would give me a bill. In two years, she saw a lot of Johnnies and asked them the same question. Maddy and I appreciated her generosity and kindness.

One Sunday in late June, I used twenty-five dollars of my college loan money to impress Maddy. I rented a 1965 turquoise Mustang from Hertz. Cool—and not yet a classic. Since I needed to drive a station wagon for deliveries, I had a driver's license, unusual for a teenager in the city, especially for someone who could never afford a car.

Now, instead of spending over an hour standing in hot, crowded subway cars headed to Far Rockaway Beach, the Irish Riviera of Queens, we went to Montauk on the tip of Long Island. There was no subway connection between

Montauk and Manhattan, so going there became a vacation, an adventure.

We played. Giggling, she covered my legs with sand while I lay on my stomach. And when I stood up, I carried her into the ocean. The water was still very cold, and she hugged my neck and pleaded with me. But I kept walking. Cold water was not going to stop me. I wanted her to know that I was fearless.

When the water was up to my chest, I stopped, and we held each other and gently rose and fell with the waves. When her legs tightened around me, I felt strong and confident, and I loved her very much.

At the end of the day, we lay on Maddy's old bedspread with our faces inches apart. When the day became gray and windy, the sand blew against us. We pulled the sides of the bedspread up over ourselves, and we became children playing under a table covered with a sheet.

Inside our special world, we told each other secrets, things we'd never say to another person. We made embarrassing confessions, because we wanted to share everything. We wanted to be vulnerable and trusting, and I never felt so safe.

"You have beautiful eyes, Jamie."

"Yours are beautiful. Golden beautiful."

"I love yours."

"They're yours."

"Always?"

"Always."

"I know. I just like to hear you say it."

"It's getting late, Maddy." I felt the blowing wind against my back and heard the sharp tapping of sand against the cooler. Behind Maddy, I held the ends of the bedspread together.

"We may become a sailboat if we don't leave soon."

"I'm so happy here."

"We'll always have today. We'll always have Montauk."

"My boyfriend's a poet."

"That's from *Casablanca*. I changed 'Paris' to 'Montauk.'"

"I never saw it."

"Humphrey Bogart tells Ingrid Bergman that she has to leave him for the fight against fascism, but they'll always have the memory of loving each other in Paris. They'll always have Paris."

"My boyfriend's very romantic, too."

"You make me romantic."

Maddy didn't say anything for a while.

"I would never leave you, Jamie. You could never make me leave you."

"I never would. Never. But this is our Paris."

"And so are Central Park and my hallway and . . ."

"You're the poet, Maddy." She always made me happy.

Suddenly she pushed the bedspread away, sat up, and looked at the ocean. She didn't say anything, and I knew to wait.

"Someday, we'll go to the other one . . . the one on the other side, and I'll wear my red beret every day for my blue-eyed boyfriend."

In 1955, I had a crew cut. In 1958, I looked like Elvis; and for a short time as a high school freshman, I had a "Detroit," which was a combination of both. Short on top, long on the sides forming a sharp "D.A." in the back. I also wore taps on the heels and toes of my shoes. When I walked up a dark street, I sounded bo-cool.

In 1963, we boys made fun of the "Mop Heads," the girls' favorite new band, because they looked like girls themselves, and we didn't like their stupid name.

"What's a Beatle? They misspelled it."

In 1965, I wanted to look like a Beatle, and Maddy brought Curl Free, a natural curl hair relaxer, to my apartment. I sat on the edge of the tub to lower my head into the sink. She wet my hair and applied the Curl Free. Rubbing it in, she sang, "No more curlicues for you."

With a towel around my neck, I sat up and we waited.

"I think my head's getting hot, Maddy." After a few more minutes, I was certain.

"My head's burning!"

Wearing jeans and socks, I quickly got into the tub under the running shower to put the fire out. After a while the burning stopped—and I had my straight hair. For a week, it was so straight that I needed Brylcreem. From then on, listening to their music was enough Beatles for me.

"Love, love me do, call me cur-li-cute," I sang off key for Maddy, who closed her eyes and covered her ears.

In the beginning of September, the unthinkable happened. We would no longer see each other—every day and night. We would not see each other for four days in a row. It was the end of summer, and we were going back to school. Second year of college for me. First year of college for her.

Sunday night was our last night together until Friday night. For the first time in our three-month carefree world, we had to stop playing and go home before 11:00 o'clock. After hugging, saying goodnight, and hugging again for the last time, I left and made it home by midnight.

The next morning, I met my ride on First Avenue. We had just picked up our last friend, Jay, on 79th Street, and after stopping for a red light on 80th Street, I saw Maddy. She was speaking with her mother in front of the beauty salon. I knew her mother worked there, but I never expected to see her. I immediately rolled the window all the way down and stuck my arm out to wave.

"Maddy!"

Hearing her name, she looked around. When she saw my waving arm, she smiled and waved her hand back and forth over her head. With her other hand, she pointed to me, and her mother waved.

"Jamie!"

The light turned green, and since we all had a 9:00 class, Anthony shifted into first gear, hit the gas hard, and we were on our way again. I continued waving until I couldn't see her anymore. Falling back into my seat, I couldn't speak. I heard my friends joke about our chance meeting.

"Gee, what a coincidence. Her standing like that on First Avenue at 7:30 in the morning. And just when we're driving by."

"Yah, and I wonder how she got that light to turn red. She must have special powers, right?"

"Yeah, how about that?"

"Hey, Lachlan. All of a sudden, you're awfully quiet back there. What's going on? You okay or what?"

"Leave him alone. He just had a vision."

"Oh, here's a good guess. Jamie, are you in love with that girl wearing the yellow dress, the one with the special powers?" They all laughed.

I couldn't laugh. It was special. It was fate. I was sure of it. And yes, I was in love, and I didn't speak until we got to school. I was trying to understand what had just happened to me. In a yellow cotton summer dress, she *was* a vision. This morning, I saw her for the very first time again—and I was lovesick.

We survived the year by meeting for an hour every Wednesday night at a diner on 78th Street and 3rd Avenue, halfway between our homes. We weren't going to lose time traveling back and forth alone. Sipping our coffee for an hour, we held hands across the table and spoke about our day without each other. Saying goodnight in her hallway for a half hour was always sweet and sad.

On other nights, we spoke on the phone. If my mother was using the phone in our studio apartment, or if our conversation was going to be unusually personal—and my mother didn't feel like sitting in the kitchen for over an hour—I went to the corner drugstore with a pocketful of nickels.

Neither one of us was usually a big phone talker, but we never ran out of things to say to each other. Once, when only one nickel was left on the phone booth shelf, she offered to call me back.

"You can't, Maddy. The owner here doesn't like it."

"Why?"

"He just doesn't. He'll throw me out and won't let me come back."

In the past, whenever the druggist heard the phone ring, he'd come out from behind the counter, slightly push open the door, and point toward the store's door and pretend he was holding a phone with the other hand.

"Go home and use your own phone. This one's for paying customers."

"Jamie, when it rings, pick it up quick."

"I can't."

"Give me the number. If you love me, you will, James."

"Nice try, Madeline."

I loved her laughter. It was contagious, so I covered the phone's mouthpiece. She wasn't going to hear me laugh. When it was safe to uncover the phone, I became very serious.

"Please. He'll never let me deliver perfume to that beautiful actress across the street again."

When I was younger, my friends and I played punchball around the corner from the drugstore. If the druggist had a delivery, he'd ask one of us to make it. One lucky day, he asked me to bring a small package to the new building, and I met an actress from a popular television show. She was beautiful . . . red-haired . . . polite . . . and generous. And she was fully, and modestly, clothed.

"Gee, what a great story, Lachlan. You should write a book about your affair someday."

"No, not that affair, Ferrara. When I do write it, I'll write it about the most beautiful woman in my life."

"If you say that Lia, that neighbor of yours . . ."

"Well, Lia is beautiful, but . . ."

"All right then, Lachlan. I'll write about the Curl Free, hot-head cry-baby James Lachlan."

I'd never been much of a phone person, but Maddy made it fun and easy. She heard me laugh that time.

For our first anniversary, we went to Southampton with two other couples—and a huge bamboo umbrella, which I borrowed from the display department at Jones & Jones, an upscale department store for women on Fifth Avenue. A friend of a friend had referred me, and I had the best summertime job of my life.

Business was slow in the summer, so the liquor shop had laid me off until September. I was very glad not to return to the Canada Dry shape-up in Queens. It was never a sure thing. I'd stand with a group of men, and the boss would point at the lucky ones who'd be helpers on trucks for the day.

"You . . . you . . . you . . . you . . ."

If you were picked, you quickly gave your social security number to the boss, and he gave you a truck number. They paid very well, but some days I wasn't picked and had to make the long trip home with nothing to show for it. I've never forgotten my social security number, though.

At Jones & Jones, I worked in the display department, where I first heard the word *gay* used to describe a homosexual man. All the employees were men—and gay—and the director refused to believe that I was *straight*.

"If his middle name is not 'Mary Sue,' I'm Hugh Hefner."

"You think everyone's gay, Ted."

"If he's not, why's he here working with us?"

"It's a summer job. He's in college and needs money. He wants to be a Spanish teacher."

"All right. A gay hombre, then."

I started to laugh and Harold turned to me.

"Show him Maddy's picture, Jamie. The one with the red beret. Go ahead." Harold thought she was beautiful. "If I were straight . . ."

"No chance of that, Harold. Okay, she's a good beard—or maybe he's 'bi.' But you know what, Harold? His . . . girlfriend . . . has a wonderful face for a mannequin model. What beautiful eyes. She's Audrey Hepburn sweet with light eyes. Can't you see her face on one of our girls?"

In the window-dressing business, you never called a mannequin a *dummy*. She was a *girl*, or a mannequin, and you never put an undressed girl in the window. If you dressed her in the window, you did it behind a sheet covering the window. Adding shoes and hats was fine for public view.

The director sent the picture of Maddy to someone in the business, but her face never made it to Fifth Avenue. But we did get the bamboo umbrella, which looked like a little straw hut on the beach, and we celebrated our anniversary in beautiful Southampton. In the evenings, we drove to the clubs in Hampton Bays, where the vacation continued with dancing and drinking.

We got home very late that Sunday night, and tired and sunburned, sitting in her hallway, I made Maddy cry. I broke up with her.

I walked along First Avenue with my ring in my closed hand. When I got home, I cried, too. I cried for Maddy who never saw it coming. I cried for myself, because I didn't see it coming, either. But something happened to me at that dance club in Hampton Bays. I noticed other girls looking at me.

When Maddy was in the bathroom, a girl asked me to dance. I said no, of course, but I couldn't believe it. A good-looking girl had asked me to dance. That was the first time any girl had ever asked me to dance. Suddenly I didn't want to be tied down. I didn't want be married like Ronnie and Cookie. Maddy had given me a new confidence in myself.

It took me one day to regret my decision, but it was too late. I called Maddy. Her mother informed me that she was visiting her cousin in New Jersey and "having a good time." She'd be back in a week.

"Please tell her I called."

"Yes."

I said goodbye and her mother hung up. She didn't say goodbye.

When Maddy returned the following Sunday afternoon, she called and left a message with my mother, and that evening we met at our diner. When she opened the door, I stood, something I had stopped doing; and before she had a chance to slide into the booth opposite me, I apologized. I had no excuse. I loved her. I asked if she ever had any crazy ideas about seeing someone else. I told her I never wanted to see anyone else again. I couldn't stop speaking, so Maddy cut me off.

"My cousin Sally fixed me up over the weekend." When I looked surprised—then angry—she slowly moved her head back and forth.

"Madd…"

"We're not going steady anymore, Jamie."

"I know…I know…but…" I was going to be calm. "Did you enjoy the date? What did you do? Did you like what's-his-name?"

What had I done to us? To myself?

"I had a good time. He was very nice. Yes, I liked him. I liked him very much."

"That was a pretty quick date, Maddy. We just broke up last weekend. Did you think of me at all?"

"We? Not we. You, Jamie, you broke us up. I thought about you breaking up with me. How much it hurt…yes, I thought about you. Now I have a question for you, Jamie. Whatever happened to, 'We'll always have today'? What does that mean to you, Jamie? Just a day on a Montauk beach? Or just a line from Casablanca you've always wanted to use? I never thought we were characters in a movie. I thought today meant every day…and everywhere."

I was trying to make her feel guilty, but that stopped me.

"No, it did. I'll always love you. I know. I know. I'm sorry I was such a jerk. I am a jerk."

It was an awful, stupid mistake, and I was angry with myself; but now I was angry with her, too.

"So what did you do on this nice date, Maddy?" I was not going to show her that I cared.

"We had two nice dates."

"Two! Why the hell…you went out twice with the same guy? Where did you go?"

"On the first date, we went danc…"

"You went dancing with some strange guy? Did you dance slow and close? Did you put your hand on his neck? Did you close your eyes?" I couldn't stop myself, because it felt good. "Did you put both arms around…?"

"Stop it, Jamie."

"What did you do next, Maddy? Make out in the backseat of his New Jersey car? He had a car, right?"

Now I didn't care if she knew I was angry. All I wanted was to hurt her. I was suffering, and she was dancing and having fun with strangers. I began to slide out of the booth to leave, but Maddy, reaching over the table and knocking over a salt shaker, grabbed my wrist.

"Why, Jamie? What does it matter now? I'm never going to see him again. I said that I liked him. I don't love him. Do you love me? Not movie love. Real love."

Suddenly I wasn't angry anymore. I felt a rush of happiness, because she wanted to hear me say that I loved her. She still loved me.

"Last week was the worst week of my life, Maddy, and I know one thing for sure. I love you, and I'll always love you."

As soon as we left the diner, we hugged for a long time in the street before I walked her home. I never mentioned New Jersey—or the second date—again. She never asked for the ring back, and I never offered it. It symbolized something new for both of us. It remained in the drawer, and that didn't matter, since we loved each other.

During our second year together, we had a good time; however, seeing Olivier's movie version of *Othello* made a lasting impression on us both. In her hallway that night, we spoke about love and jealousy, pride and anger for a long time.

"To be once in doubt is to be resolved."

Othello's warning to Iago had meaning for both of us. We didn't realize it then, but we had doubts about each other. In 1967, we stopped seeing each other. We never argued. One morning, I called Maddy and no one answered the phone. I never called back—and she never called me. Just like that, our two years together and our promise of loving each other forever ended in silence.

It was dawn and Rachel had thirty minutes of sleep before her alarm clock would ring. This time tomorrow, we'd be back in New York. I hadn't slept at all. How could I? I also remembered the conversation I had had with Ronnie. He lived in Brooklyn, and I hadn't seen him in several years. At the beginning of last winter, I met him and his daughter at the Central Park Zoo. I knew Cookie and he were married, but I hadn't heard about his little girl, Caitlin. Ronnie was really married now.

As old friends do, we spoke about the golden days, the good times and the better times. We spoke about our friends. While I was in college, Ronnie had kept in touch with everyone. Charlie had joined the army and immediately was sent to Viet Nam.

"Poor Charlie. Has he sent any letters home?"

"Not to us. Did you hear about Butchie's heart attack?"

"No. Oh, poor Butchie. What the hell! How's he doing?"

"Pretty good now, I think. He said he lost a lot of weight, and he sounds good on the phone. He's still living with his parents. Still wants to be a famous singer and still arguing with Archie. Those guys should get married."

"They are funny. What's Archie doing?"

"Working at the brewery with his father."

"We had a good time growing up, Ronnie. Great friends."

"Yeah, we did. Life on the block was the best. Lots more complicated today. How's Daniel doing?"

"He lives in Jersey, because he's an engineer out there. And he's getting married."

"No, who is she?"

"He met her at Princeton. She's getting her doctorate in American literature. Emily Dickinson, I think. She writes poetry, too. Really a nice girl."

"Smart girl."

"Yeah, Daniel met his match."

"Catholic or Jewish?"

"Buddhist."

"Buddhist!"

"She's Chinese."

"Chinese! You're kidding."

"No, her parents are Chinese, but she was born here."

"Chinese. Daniel always had to be different. And I know you're the best man, right? No big surprise there. What about you, Jamie? Getting married anytime soon, too?"

"I'm . . . we're getting serious; in fact, I'm meeting my mother today to pick out a birthday gift for my girlfriend. My mother and Rachel are good friends already."

At some point during our conversation, we knew we had nothing left to say; we no longer had anything in common. I pinched Caitlin's cheek and shook Ronnie's hand. He was going to show her the bears. I was going to walk north through the park near Fifth Avenue. Then Ronnie looked confused and surprised me.

"Did you know that Maddy called you a few times after your break-up?"

"No, we never spoke again."

"Remember receiving strange calls a few years ago? No one on the other end?"

"Maybe. I don't know."

"You didn't know who it was?"

"Wrong numbers. People hang up all the time."

"That was Maddy."

"Maddy? Maddy? Why? How do you know, Ronnie?"

"Back then, Cookie and Maddy still talked once in a while." Ronnie and I had double dated twice.

"So why didn't she say something, Ronnie? I said hello. Why didn't she answer?"

"She thought you'd know. She wanted to hear you say 'Maddy.'"

Lying in our Roman room far from home, I remembered every word of that conversation with Ronnie in the park. All of it was still very close to me, and remembering it made me very sad and even lonely. I listened to Rachel's light breathing, which made me feel better, because we were going to be different. We weren't teenagers in love. We weren't kids.

Acknowledgments

For their inspiration, motivation, and professional and artistic support, I thank Jerry Ahern, Howard Alexander, Lynn Breindel, Bob Capazzo Photography, Georgine Capazzo, Hsin-cheng Chuang, Nancy Deslandes, Alan Jaffe, Danny Lopriore, Stephen Meli, Patrick Niland, Andi Rosenthal, Julia Santangelo, Georganne Serico, Louis Serico, and Natalie Turner of freelancepermissions.com.

For his excellent cover design, I thank Stephen Harry.

For their editorial support—and unyielding patience—I thank Kathy Barbagallo, David Breindel, John Thomas Clark, Bob Liftig, Carolyn Moen, Melissa Willard Parent, Joanna Shubin, and Roberta Silman.

And for too many reasons to list here, I thank Christina Burk, Tara Carmody, Geneviève Leonard , and Jonathan Shubin.

Credits

Angel Baby
Words and Music by Rose Hamlin
© 1960 (Renewed 1988) EMI LONGITUDE MUSIC
All Rights Reserved International Copyright Secured Used by Permission
Reprinted by Permission of Hal Leonard Corporation

Good Golly Miss Molly
Words and Music by Robert Blackwell and John Marascalco
Copyright (c) 1957 Jondora Music, Robin Hood Music Co. and Cedos Music
Copyright Renewed
International Copyright Secured All Rights Reserved
Reprinted by Permission of Hal Leonard Corporation, Robin Hood Music Co. and Cedos Music.

I GOT YOU BABE
Words and Music by SONNY BONO
Copyright © 1965 (Renewed) COTILLION MUSIC, INC. and CHRIS-MARC MUSIC
All Rights Administered by COTILLION MUSIC, INC
All Rights Reserved Used by Permission

Poison Ivy
Words and Music by Jerry Leiber and Mike Stoller
Copyright (C) 1959 Sony/ATV Music Publishing LLC
Copyright Renewed
All Rights Administered by Sony/ATV Music Publishing LLC, 8 Music Square West, Nashville, TN 37203
International Copyright Secured All Rights Reserved
Reprinted by Permission of Hal Leonard Corporation

About the Author

Please visit www.RichardLeonard.net

and

www.RichardLeonard.net page on Facebook